The
TEMPTATION
of
DIRTY
SECRETS

The *TEMPTATION* *of* *DIRTY* *SECRETS*

USA TODAY BESTSELLING AUTHOR

HOLLY RENEE

FOR UNCLE KENNY

For always supporting me.

You're still not allowed to read this.

CHAPTER 1

FRANKIE

Everyone saw what they wanted to see.

The Clermonts' perfect daughter.

Beck's little sister.

The poor girl that got assaulted.

The one who was so desperate that she was trying to hook up with all of her brother's friends.

I had become an accumulation of these titles they had given me.

They were whispered in the halls at school and stared at me in the faces of everyone I passed.

They all thought they knew exactly who I was, but they didn't have a clue.

I didn't have a fucking clue.

But they had gotten a front-row seat to my heartbreak. They had all seen what Lucas had done to me on the screens of their phones, and they all still gossiped about the way I had told Olly I loved him at that party and how he could barely look me in the eye.

And the assumptions they were making were starting to

eat at me. With every passing second, they became more real.

Olly was my weakness, and he had become my strength.

He had become my safe place and my crutch, and suddenly, I didn't know who I was without him.

I knew the thoughts that were running through my head were irrational, but that didn't make them feel any less real.

I had fallen for Olly. I had given him more of myself than I had ever given anyone, and it wasn't enough.

God, I hated that word.

When would it ever be enough? Was I a good enough daughter? Had I apologized enough to Beck? Had I hated myself enough for what happened with Lucas? Had I tried hard enough to hang on to Olly?

Enough seemed to be the goal that was always in the back of my mind that I could never quite reach.

None of it was enough.

I knew it the moment I opened my eyes while I was still in Olly's arms. Every bit of courage I had been desperately trying to build up fell away as a single thought ran through my head.

I didn't want Olly to love me because he felt like he had to.

He was the best guy I knew, and he would give everything up if that was what I wanted. He had broken my heart, but he would do whatever it took to fix it if I let him.

But that would never be enough for him or for me.

And that was so unhealthy. Everything about us had been from the beginning. I was his secret, he was my obsession, and even though he had been such an integral part in helping me heal, what we had become was toxic for both of us.

It didn't matter that he had already broken my heart when he walked away. Me coming back, me coming here to his place, it had done nothing but fuel his need to protect me.

But I didn't need him to protect me anymore. Not any of them.

I felt trapped by the idea of him constantly feeling the need to save me. I had to learn to save myself.

CHAPTER 2
OLLY

I felt like I was going out of my mind.

It had been less than a week since Frankie left my apartment without a word. A week of texts and calls, and I couldn't take it anymore.

The phone rang over and over as I paced around our small kitchen.

It went to Frankie's voice mail, but I immediately called back.

I was preparing myself for her not to answer again. My hands shook as I thought about what I was going to do. If she wouldn't answer me, then I had no choice but to call Beck.

I had to know that she was okay.

"Hello." Her voice was soft, and she sounded so tired.

"Frankie." I breathed her name with relief. God, I hadn't realized just how bad it was fucking me up that she was refusing to talk to me.

It was destroying me that she left after everything.

"What do you need, Olly? I'm about to walk into English."

Fuck. She was at school. I hadn't even thought about that. I just knew that I couldn't take her ignoring me anymore.

"I just want to talk to you." I ran my fingers over the counter. "I need to apologize."

"There is nothing for you to apologize for. We had our summer, we hurt each other, and now it is time for us to move on."

I shook my head because she was wrong. I had been so fucking wrong.

"You know that's a lie."

She laughed bitterly before she said the next words. "What I know is that I can't do this anymore, Olly. I can't keep allowing someone to have this much power over me. I'm not going to hand over the power for you to hurt me again."

Her words hit me in my gut, and I couldn't breathe.

That was the last thing I wanted. I didn't want to hurt her. I fucking hated the fact that I had done so already.

I had known the moment I had given her up for the sake of anyone other than us I had made a mistake. Fuck, I knew it long before that. But seeing it in her eyes staring back at me, I couldn't hide from it anymore.

I was in love with her, and nothing else mattered.

I was an idiot for believing that it ever did.

"What can I do, Frankie? Do you want me to tell Beck that this is what I want? Do you want me to come home?"

"Don't be insane."

I could hear people around her, and I hated that we were having this conversation like this. I wished she had never left. I wished she had fucking talked to me.

"There is nothing to tell Beck, Olly. You're in California, and I'm here. Please don't make this harder than it has to be."

She was pushing me away. I could hear the edge of panic in her voice, and I knew that this was her way of protecting herself.

I fucking hurt her, and it was too much.

Fear punched me in the chest. I tried to think of the right words, the right thing to do that would save us. It was a battle inside myself between what I knew was good for her and what I felt.

But I knew with certainty that I loved Frankie Clermont. I loved her and she loved me too, but I broke her.

"Just tell me what to do." I was fucking begging her, but I knew that I would do whatever she told me to do. I would do whatever it took to make it up to her.

"Just let me move on, Olly. This isn't healthy," she whispered, and I knew that she was right. What we were doing to each other wasn't good for either of us, but it didn't make me want her any less. "I just need to be able to be okay on my own."

I didn't know how to answer her without lying to her. I wanted that for her too, but it was also the last thing I wanted. I couldn't imagine not being a part of her life. I didn't know how not to love her.

"Okay." I nodded my head and clamped my eyes closed. "I'll let you get to class." We were both silent for a long moment. "You'll call me if you need me?"

"Yeah." Her answer was a lie of her own.

I broke her, and I didn't know what to do.

CHAPTER 3
FRANKIE

One Year Later

I pushed through the crowd of people and made my way up to the bar. I smiled as I caught the attention of my favorite bartender, and he grinned while tossing his towel onto his shoulder.

"What can I do for you, Frankie?"

"Tequila on the rocks with a squeeze of lime."

He laid his elbows against the bar and leaned forward until his face was close to mine. Only a few inches separated us. "Did you notice how packed we are tonight?"

"I did." I nodded and looked to my right where some guy was laughing obnoxiously. "That's what took me so long to get up here. I didn't think I was ever going to make it through the crowd."

"Did you stop and think maybe Greg isn't going to serve me tonight since there are so many people around, and I'm barely a day over nineteen?" He cocked his eyebrow, and I could feel people around us watching us. Not because they were interested, but because they wanted him to hurry and serve them a drink.

"Nope." I shook my head and matched his position. "I'm pretty sure it's impossible for you to tell me no."

He only hesitated for a second before his lips lifted on the side in a cocky smile. "That's the truth. I couldn't tell you no if I wanted to." He chuckled as I handed him a twenty-dollar bill. He grabbed a glass, filled it with ice and a generous amount of tequila before sliding me my drink. His gaze trailed over my face before they stopped on my lips.

"You forgot my lime."

"I didn't forget." He reached for a lime and ran it over the rim of my glass before dropping it inside. "I just wanted to look at you for a few more seconds before you disappeared."

Heat bloomed in my chest, and I knew he could see the blush crossing my face. If I hadn't been thinking about how I had kissed him outside of the bar the week before, I definitely was now.

I shouldn't have done it. It was one of those don't shit where you eat kind of scenarios since this had become my favorite place to drink, but I had one too many tequilas and his face was just a touch too handsome.

"You're too good to me, Greg." I smiled but tried to hide the anxiety that was creeping in. I wasn't interested in kissing him again. I wasn't interested in doing anything with him other than being his friend.

"Be safe." He nodded toward the crowd, and I saluted him before giving him a wink. He was always trying to watch over me, to make sure I was okay, and I should have been flattered by the fact. But I wasn't.

Because it reminded me too much of him, and I hated anything that reminded me of him.

I smiled and turned around with my drink in my hand. I was about to walk away when I bumped into someone and knocked my drink between our chests.

"Oh my God. I'm so sorry." I stumbled over my words as I fumbled for napkins off the bar behind me and tried to blot at the liquid that was now coating his shirt.

"It's okay." He chuckled and took one of the napkins from my hand. "I didn't get much on me."

I looked up just as he took the napkin and wiped it across my own shirt. The tequila was soaking through my white tank top and the work he was doing wasn't going to make one bit of difference.

But I didn't stop him.

I couldn't have if I wanted to because I was too busy noticing how his eyes were the same color as my favorite shade of the ocean, and how his white button-up molded to his chest.

"I didn't even see you standing there. I'm so sorry. This place is so crowded tonight." I straightened out my shirt that was now clinging to my chest as he tossed the soiled napkins on the counter.

"It's not a big deal," he reassured me as he smiled. "What were you drinking? I'll get you another."

"You don't have to do that." I shook my head, but he was moving the few steps toward the bar and lifting his hand in the air.

"It's the least I can do." The way he was looking at me forced me to look away. He looked at me like he saw something more than what I was. Something that could be more than this moment.

He was a perfect stranger, but he was looking at me like I was the best thing he had seen all night.

"Why's that?"

"Well, you say you didn't see me, but I haven't been able to take my eyes off you." His gaze skimmed over my face. "I was coming over here to talk to you and caused you to spill your drink."

I looked back at him and searched his face as he smiled. He was handsome, there was no denying that, but my stomach didn't flutter as he spoke. If anything, listening to what he was saying did nothing but make me crave that feeling. A feeling I had been missing for far longer than I liked to admit. "Tequila on the rocks with lime."

"Okay." There was a low rumble in his voice, and the way he smiled was like he knew something that I didn't. He thought that my drink order was a sign that I was interested in him, but I wasn't. I hadn't been interested in anyone since him.

He nodded toward Greg and caught his attention, and he stopped in front of him before his gaze slid to me. "Can I get a tequila on the rocks?"

"With lime," Greg finished for him before he could.

"Exactly." He chuckled and turned to look back at me. "What's your name?"

"Frankie." I tucked my hair behind my ear before sliding my hands into my back pockets. "You?"

"Ben."

"It's nice to meet you." I felt awkward standing there waiting for my drink, and if I wasn't in desperate need of tequila, I probably would have already bounced.

"You too. You go to the university?"

"Yeah." I nodded and watched as Greg made my drink. "Business major."

"Me too." He chuckled and rapped his knuckles against the bar. "I can't believe I've never seen you before."

"Maybe you have and just didn't realize." I shrugged. I saw hundreds of people at this damn school every day, and I could barely remember any of their faces.

"No. Trust me. I would remember."

My skin heated, and I opened my mouth to respond just as Greg slid my drink in front of Ben and looked at me. "You okay?"

"Yeah." I flushed with embarrassment as I nodded.

"Make sure you come to see me before you leave."

Ben looked back and forth between us, but I tried not to look at either of them.

"I will." I nodded again and took a long drink of my tequila.

It burned my throat with a deliciousness that I craved.

I stepped away from the bar, and Ben followed me.

"You got a thing with the bartender?"

His question annoyed me, but I tried to let it roll off my back. "I don't have a thing with anyone."

I pushed through the crowd, and he was at my back the whole time. I should have been flattered by his interest in me, but I couldn't force myself to be.

I made it to the table where my friends were sitting and took my empty seat. Ben grabbed a chair from the table next to us and pulled it up next to me.

Dawn raised her eyebrows at me in question as she watched him settle in beside me, and I shrugged my shoulders and tried to stop myself from rolling my eyes.

I met Dawn on the day we moved into our apartment

together, and we hit it off instantly. She was my go-to girl when it came to escaping my own thoughts and losing ourselves out at the bar.

I smiled over at Ben who was watching me and pulled my phone out of my pocket. The music was blaring in the bar, so I didn't feel the overwhelming need to make small talk, but I still felt awkward.

There was a text from Josie on my phone, and I winced as I read it.

Josie: What are you doing tonight? I feel like we've barely talked all week.

That was because we hadn't. The university was only about a twenty-minute drive back to my parents' house, and even though I still spent most of my time there, sometimes it became overwhelming.

Everything reminded me of Olly, and when I heard Beck talk about him, I had to smile and pretend like he didn't matter to me. I had to act like I hadn't spent the entire last year trying to force myself to think about anything other than him.

I had barely seen him over the past year, but it didn't matter. Every time I did, it was like no time had passed. He was still the boy I was in love with, and I was still the girl who couldn't have him.

I was the girl who pushed him away.

And now he was in love with someone else.

"Do you come here a lot?"

"What?" I looked up from my phone to Ben, and I almost forgot he was sitting there.

"This bar." He motioned around us. "Do you come here a lot?"

"Oh. Yeah." I nodded. "It's the best place to get tequila when you're only nineteen."

He laughed and rubbed his hand over the smattering of hair on his jaw. That one simple move reminded me of Olly, and a deep ache pressed against my chest.

"I guess you have a good point there. What year are you?"

"Freshman. You?" I nodded in his direction. He was definitely older than me, but he wasn't too much older.

"Senior."

"Oh, Frankie!" Dawn leaned forward and rubbed her hands together playfully. "It looks like you have caught yourself a daddy."

Ben blanched and stuttered over his next words. "I don't have any kids."

I rolled my eyes as Dawn laughed, and leaned closer to him so he could hear me. "That's not what she means. She's calling you a daddy because you're older."

"Oh." He wrinkled his brow, and honestly, I could tell he was going to be a ball of fun.

"I'm taking it you've never dated a younger girl before." I didn't know why I said that. He obviously wasn't dating me, and I had no plans to change that. Guys like Ben reminded me too much of the guys in Clermont Bay, the guys I was forced to spend my last year of high school with while I was miserable, and I had no interest in spending even more time with them.

It didn't matter how handsome he was.

Nothing seemed to matter because every time I thought I could move past Olly, I couldn't. I just compared every single move they made, everything about them, to him.

And it wasn't fucking fair.

"No." He shook his head. "This would be a first for me."

"Whoa, whoa, whoa." I lifted my glass of tequila and downed the rest of the clear liquid. "No one said there was a this."

He winced, and I instantly felt bad. "That's not what I meant. I wasn't saying…"

"I'm just busting your balls." I smiled and set down my glass. "So, Business Major Ben, are you local, or did you move here for college?"

"I moved here." He pressed his elbows into his knees and leaned forward. "I'm originally from Texas."

"I thought I heard a little twang in there." I tapped my ear, and he laughed.

"I do everything in my power to get rid of that twang and everything I left in Texas." He smiled softly, but it was hiding something beneath that I couldn't quite place.

It made me more interested in him than I had been in anyone in a long time.

"What about you? You a local girl?"

"I am." I nodded and gripped the sides of my seat. "My parents live a few miles north of here."

"They on the coast?"

"Yeah." I nodded.

"That's awesome." His gaze ran over my face. "I love the ocean. The sounds, the smell."

I nodded as I could practically imagine what he was saying. "Me too. It's my favorite place in the world."

"I wouldn't have left here either."

I couldn't tell him that the reason I didn't leave was that I had been hoping and praying that my staying would mean that Olly would eventually come back. Even though I knew

Clermont Bay was the last place he wanted to be, deep down I was holding out hope that he would come back for me.

I was the one who had pushed him away. I told him that this thing between us couldn't work, and I knew that was the truth. But I also knew that deep down, I still craved every part of him.

And that was fucking pathetic.

I didn't have time to constantly think about Olly.

Beck had been working hard with my father over the last year, and he had taken so much of my father's responsibilities on that I didn't have to shoulder any of them.

And I knew Beck did that for me. He did that because he wanted me to go to college and live the dream, as he quoted to me often. But I always used my family as an excuse for why I stayed.

My parents were both doing well; my dad was smiling more now that he had Beck in the position to help him, and I liked to pretend that they needed me more than they did.

Because if they needed me, then I wasn't wasting my life by staying here. If they needed me, then I wasn't as big of a fool as I truly knew I was.

Because I had pushed Olly away, and even though nothing really was, I felt like I was falling apart.

I pushed Olly away because I knew he wasn't good for me, but I desperately wanted him to be.

"I'm actually going home this weekend for this little get-together at my parents' house." *What the hell are you doing, Frankie?* "Do you want to come with me?"

He grinned, deep and genuine, and I wished it affected me more than it did. "A moment ago you were giving me shit over there not being a this" —he motioned his hand back and forth between us— "and now you want to take me home to meet the parents?"

I winced because he was right, but there was no going back now. "My parents won't actually be there. But you will meet my older brother, which is actually worse. Take it or leave it."

"Take it." He watched me and searched my eyes. "I'm definitely going to take it."

CHAPTER 4
OLLY

"This is so good, Carson." Jordan looked up at my friend and smiled before glancing back at me. "Thank you for cooking."

"You're welcome." He smiled back at her even though he didn't like her. I would even dare to say that he hated her even though he would never admit it.

He had hated her from the moment he met her.

"What time do we have to be at workouts?" I avoided his gaze and took the last bite off my plate.

"Thirty minutes." He dropped his dishes into the sink, then looked back over at me. "Be ready in ten."

"I'll be ready." I turned back to Jordan and pushed some of her soft brown hair over her shoulder. She smiled up at me like she always did, like I was the best thing that ever happened to her, and guilt clawed at my chest.

Because even though I really liked Jordan, she would never be Frankie.

And that was so fucked up.

I was more than aware of that fact. It had been a year

since Frankie and I were last together. Over a year since she ran out of my apartment like she couldn't get away from me fast enough, but I still couldn't get her out of my head.

I couldn't make my chest quit aching when I thought about her every time I kissed Jordan. I was doing everything in my power to move on from her, but it didn't seem to matter.

Everything reminded me of her. Everything Jordan did, I compared to her.

It didn't matter that I was using Jordan to drown out my need for Frankie. It wasn't intentional, or at least it hadn't been in the beginning, but I slipped into that vice so easily.

Frankie was the person I never stopped looking for.

I didn't know how to move past it, past her, and part of me knew that I didn't want to. Not really. I wanted to cling to the feeling that she gave me. A feeling that I hadn't been able to find anywhere else.

"You want me to walk you out to your car?"

"No. I'll be fine." She shook her head just as Carson left the room. "I'd rather spend a few minutes alone before I go."

"I know, but I can't be late." My chest tightened even harder. It wasn't a lie, but it also wasn't the whole truth. But I couldn't tell her that I had seen a post Frankie made on Instagram earlier, and now even my normal tricks to clear my mind of her weren't working. "Coach will have my ass."

"I know." She nodded, but I could see the hurt in her eyes. She knew that something was off with me. Jordan and I had been dating for less than six months, but Frankie wasn't something we talked about anymore. I had told her about Frankie once on a drunken night when I was pushing her away, but she's never brought her up since. "I'll see you later?"

"Yeah." I leaned forward and pressed my lips to her forehead. "I'll text you as soon as I get back."

She wrapped her hands around my neck, pulling me down until my lips met hers, and she kissed me like she was scared it wouldn't happen again. It always felt like that, like I was kissing her goodbye.

I pulled away from her when it was clear that she wasn't going to, and she looked up at me with such sad eyes. That was something that she and Frankie had in common. They were both so fucking expressive with one simple look.

But while Jordan's filled me with guilt, a look from Frankie could cut me to my core.

Jordan walked out the door, and I ran my fingers through my hair before I stood. It took me no time to get my gear on even though my head still felt like it was clouded by a million different thoughts. I had no interest in going to workouts.

Fuck. I didn't want to do anything, but pick up my phone and try to call Frankie.

My hand shook around my phone as I stared down at her name, and it took everything inside of me not to call her. I clicked it off before sliding it into my shorts and walking out of my room.

Carson and Garrett were waiting on me in the living room when I walked out, and I tried to push away all thoughts of her as I faced my friends.

"What's up, fucker?" Garrett tossed his Gatorade bottle from one hand to the next. Garrett was on our team, and at our apartment more than not. Most of the time it felt like he lived here.

"Nothing."

"Told you." Carson grabbed his bag and headed toward the door without another word.

"You told him what?" I followed behind him, grabbing my bag along the way. Neither one of them answered me until we had climbed into Garrett's truck, and he pulled out of the parking lot.

"Carson just said that you were moping around a bit today."

"Correction." Carson held up his finger. "I told him that you were being a moody bitch."

I rolled my eyes at both of them and pulled my phone back out of my pocket. "I am not being moody. I have a fucking headache."

"You sure do." Carson nodded, and it grated on my nerves.

"Just say whatever it is you want to say, Carson. I'm seriously not in the mood." I clicked on Instagram and scrolled through my feed absentmindedly.

"Why are you still doing this bullshit with Jordan when you're still not over Frankie?"

"Considering I've barely talked to or seen Frankie in the last year, I'd say I'm fucking over her." It was a lie that neither one of us believed.

"Am I going to meet this legendary Frankie when we go to Clermont Bay this weekend?"

"Absolutely."

"Probably not," Carson and I answered at the exact same time.

Carson turned in his seat to get a better look at me. "Do you honestly think we're going to go back, and you're not going to see her?"

I shrugged my shoulders because that was exactly what I

thought. "She's away for college, and from what Josie tells me, partying all the time. I highly doubt she'll be in Clermont Bay." The thought alone ate at me. I was always so damn worried about her, and I wasn't there. I wasn't there, and she was moving on.

"You're delusional." He searched my face, and I knew he was looking for whatever it was I wasn't telling him. But he wouldn't find it. I had become an expert in locking away my feelings for Frankie. At least from others.

Most days I felt like I was dying on the inside without her, but I could hide it. I had to hide it.

"Well." I shrugged again. "We'll either see her or we won't."

"It doesn't matter to you either way." I couldn't tell if it was a statement or a question.

"It doesn't."

"Uh-huh," he said that so sarcastically. "And I bet that when you see her, you won't be affected by her in the least."

"Correct." I stared him down and tried to get him to drop it. I wasn't in the mood to talk about Frankie. I wasn't strong enough.

"And I bet you won't be bothered at all by the fact that she apparently has a boyfriend now?"

His words hit me directly in my chest, and I felt like I couldn't breathe. Thoughts of her with someone else flashed through my mind and hit me like a train as my hands began to shake at my sides. I knew that wasn't fair. I was with Jordan. I had been with Jordan, and I couldn't expect Frankie to just be alone.

I didn't expect her to, but fuck, I don't know. I also didn't like to think about her being with anyone else. I had avoided that thought like the fucking plague.

In my head, Frankie was still mine. It didn't matter that I hadn't talked to her in what felt like forever, and it had been months since I smelled the soft coconut scent of her skin.

Hell, the last time I saw her, she practically acted like she didn't know me at all. But she did. She knew me better than anyone else.

And she still felt like mine.

"Shit. I shouldn't have said anything."

I blinked up at Carson because I had honestly forgotten that he was even there. "No. It's fine." I could barely manage to get the words out.

"It's not fine." He shook his head. "Nothing about this whole damn thing is fine. You should go home and demand that Frankie talk to you."

Demand she talk to me. I wished it were that easy. If I could simply demand that she talk to me, then I wouldn't be here right now. Because I had tried. Over and over, and Frankie didn't want to talk to me.

She had made that perfectly clear through the unanswered calls and one-word text message replies.

I wished that I could just hold her face in my hands and demand that she look at me and actually see me for the first time in what felt like forever.

I wanted her to see and hear how badly I missed her.

I couldn't grasp all the thoughts that were flashing through my head. Was she even the same Frankie that I knew? Had she changed so much that maybe she didn't think about me the way I still thought about her?

Maybe that was a good thing.

Frankie deserved to move on. Even if I couldn't. She deserved to be happy in whatever way she could.

She had told me so herself.

She was trying to move on, and I had to let her.

But that didn't mean that it still hadn't felt like a betrayal. Every time I touched Jordan, the betrayal I felt ate at me a little more and more.

Frankie wasn't even talking to me anymore, and I still felt like I was betraying her every day. But she was leaving me with no choice but to force myself to move on from her.

I fucked up when I hurt her. I hurt her, and did nothing but push her away.

We had been each other's secrets, and she deserved to be my truth. She always had.

"What would you like me to say to her?" I rubbed my hand over the back of my neck as we pulled into the school parking lot. I spotted half our team climbing out of their cars, and this was the last damn place I wanted to be. "Nothing is different between us. There isn't a damn thing for either one of us to say."

"Then you're a bigger idiot than I thought."

CHAPTER 5

FRANKIE

I felt like I had just fallen asleep when my phone rang, but as I felt around for the blaring thing, I noticed the time on my clock.

Two-oh-five in the morning.

I blinked past the brightness of my screen and hit Answer before pressing my phone to my ear.

"Hello." I let my eyes fall back closed, and I was almost back asleep when I heard his voice come through the phone.

"Fuck. Are you asleep?"

"Olly?" I knew it was him, but it had been so damn long since I talked to him that I felt a bit shocked at hearing his voice.

"Yeah." He chuckled softly. "I'm sorry. I didn't mean to wake you."

My heart hammered in my chest, and every trace of the heaviness that threatened to pull me back to sleep fell away in an instant.

"No. It's okay." I sat up in bed and pulled my knees against my chest. "I was just shocked to hear your voice."

He was quiet for another moment. "I know. I probably shouldn't have called."

"I'm glad you did," I hurried to reassure him before he could get off the phone. I felt like I had been ignoring him for so long that I couldn't remember why this wasn't a good idea.

One small whisper of his voice was pure temptation. It was like a dirty secret in the dead of the night, and no one could see us. No one was here to tell me that still wanting him was wrong.

And me wanting him was the only real truth that I knew. Everything else felt like I was faltering, pretending, guessing my way through life, but he had never felt like that. Even when I knew we weren't good for each other, he was real.

"I'm glad you finally answered." He was quiet for a long moment, and I didn't reply because, what was there to say? I couldn't tell him that wasn't the truth when we both knew damn well that it was. "Carson and I are coming to town this weekend. Are you going to be there, or will you be at school?"

I bit down on my bottom lip as I thought about my stupid fucking plan to invite Ben along for the trip. It had felt like a good idea at the time, but I was regretting it now.

"Yeah. I'll be there." I nodded even though he couldn't see it, and ran my hand over my sheets. "Josie would kill me if I missed Beck's birthday party."

"Same." He chuckled softly, and my thighs tightened at the sound. "Apparently being across the country wasn't a good enough excuse to miss it."

"Did you need an excuse to miss it?" I knew I shouldn't have asked the question because I really didn't want to know his answer.

"I don't know." There was fumbling on his end of the line, and I tried to imagine what he was doing. "I honestly didn't think you'd want to see me there. Not after the last time..."

When I had done everything in my power to pretend like he wasn't important to me.

"You're still my friend, Olly." Saying his name out loud felt forbidden on my tongue. I hadn't said it in so long because I knew what those two damn syllables could do to me.

"Am I? We don't feel much like friends anymore."

I didn't know how to answer him because he was right. We didn't feel like friends. It was as if suddenly, we were strangers again.

I was still in love with a boy who had become a stranger to me, and I didn't know how to stop.

"You'll always be my friend, Olly. Things have just been..." I hesitated because I didn't want to give too much of myself away. If I finished that sentence, if I told him how hard things had been for me when I knew he had moved on, I would be handing things over to him that I promised I never would again.

"Fucking miserable." He huffed as my chest ached, and I could imagine him running his fingers through his hair as he overthought everything he was saying. "I've been fucking miserable without you."

I slammed my eyes closed and tried to block out his words. I tried not to let them have the kind of effect on me that I already knew they would have.

"I can't do this."

"Can't do what?" He sounded so desperate. "All we're doing is having a conversation."

"No." I shook my head and pulled my sheet against my chest. "What we're doing is hurting each other."

Because he had hurt me. Completely and irrevocably, and I couldn't give him that power again. I was so tired of letting others have power over me.

"You're the one who walked out on me." His voice was so somber, and I would have felt bad if anger didn't flush every surface of my skin.

"And you're the one who made a promise that you would have nothing to do with me again."

"I broke that promise, didn't I?"

"You seem to break a lot of promises." That was a low blow, and I knew it. I knew what Olly and I had been getting into when we started.

"I didn't make you any promises, Frankie. We knew we couldn't have any promises between us."

"Just secrets," I whispered, and I hated how battered I felt. It didn't matter how much time had passed between us, how long it had been since I heard his voice, it all came flooding back to me with no effort. "Do you make promises to your girlfriend?" I pushed the anger forward and tried with everything I had to get it to overtake the heartbreak. "Is she asleep beside you right now or are you hiding me again?"

He didn't answer at first, and for a long moment, I didn't think he was going to.

"I heard that you've got yourself a boyfriend."

Ben wasn't my boyfriend, not even close, but there was no way in hell I was going to let Olly know that. Especially when I could hear the jealousy in his voice. "Is that an issue?"

"Of course, it's a fucking issue," he growled, and I pushed my thighs together at the sound.

"Is that why you're calling me? You're upset that I'm with someone else?"

"Don't do that, Frankie." I could hear his irritation dripping from his voice. "You know that I have tried to call you over and over, and you haven't wanted anything to do with me. I just…"

I pushed the guilt away and clung to my anger. "You what? You get to go fuck whoever you want. You get to fuck that girl that you were supposedly just friends with when I came to visit you, but I'm not supposed to do the same? I hate to tell you this, Olly, but you don't have to hear about a guy being my boyfriend for me to be fucking him."

It was a lie. A huge fucking lie.

Because despite how hard I was trying to act, I hadn't gotten over Olly in any way. Not emotionally and not physically. He was fucking his girlfriend like I had never mattered at all, and I could barely bring myself to touch another man.

"Don't say shit like that, Frankie. I don't want to think about you with anyone else." I could hear the anger in his voice, and I was grateful. Let him be angry.

"And you think I do? Do you really think I want to be reminded of how easily you moved on all the time?"

"I haven't moved on. I waited for you, and you're the one who told me you didn't want this. You're the one who told me to find someone else."

"And clearly you have. You're dating someone else, Olly. You've been dating her."

"And every time I close my eyes and touch her, I think about you."

I couldn't breathe as he spoke. His words were faint and reckless, and I knew that I shouldn't have drank them down as if it was the most honest thing I had ever heard.

"Olly."

"It's true." There was rustling on his end of the phone, and I pressed my back against my pillows as I tried to calm my racing heart.

"I haven't talked to you in forever, and now you're calling me to tell me that... that you..."

"That I still imagine your face when my cock is in my hand. That I can't get off without thinking about the way you smell, the way you taste. That you fucked me up so badly that no one else compares to you."

I swallowed hard and tried to keep the emotion and lust from filling my voice. "If Jordan isn't doing it for you, you can always find someone else that's better in bed."

"It doesn't have a fucking thing to do with that and you know it."

I bit down on my bottom lip as he spoke.

"Jordan doesn't do it for me because I'm not in fucking love with Jordan."

Don't say it. Don't say it.

"I can't love her because I'm still in love with you."

I knew he could hear my harsh breathing through the phone, but I had no way of stopping it. I didn't know what to say. I didn't know how to lie to him and save myself.

"Tell me you don't love me too, and we can hang up right now. Tell me you don't love me, and I'll let you go be happy as you fucking want to with your new boyfriend."

I chewed on the side of my thumb as I tried to gather the courage to lie to him. It was just a few simple words. "I can't."

He took a sharp breath, and I knew he was going to say something that I wouldn't recover from.

"But that doesn't mean anything."

"The fuck it doesn't," he growled. "What do you want me to do, Frankie?"

He was saying the things that I had wanted to hear for so long, but it still wasn't enough. Not after everything. "There's nothing for you to do. You are in California, and you have a girlfriend. We are bad for each other, Olly. Nothing is going to happen between us."

"We both know that is a lie."

"I don't."

"Yes. You do." Every word was perfectly clear. "Can I FaceTime you? I need to see you."

My heart rate spiked, and I ran my fingers through my hair. "That's not a good idea."

He didn't care about my answer. My phone started beeping, notifying me that he was FaceTiming me, and my finger shook as it hovered over the Answer button. I knew that I shouldn't. If I were smart, I would have hung up the damn phone and gone right back to sleep.

But I was never smart when it came to Olly.

That was the problem.

I pressed Answer, and a heaviness instantly hit my chest as soon as his face came into view. He was laying in his bed, just like me, and his gaze ran over every part of me that he could see through the phone.

I turned on my side with my head resting on my pillow. "If I had known you were going to call me in the middle of the night, I would have dressed better for bed."

He shook his head softly. "You're fucking gorgeous."

"Olly, what are we doing?"

His hair was disheveled and falling in his face, and I knew he had probably been running his fingers through it. It made my own hand itch to do the same.

"I just want to look at you." His tongue ran over his bottom lip. "The last time I was in town you barely let me catch a glance of you before you disappeared."

"The last time you were in town, I couldn't handle seeing you."

His gaze was on fire as he stared back at me. It didn't matter that it was dark on both of our ends, I didn't need light to see the way he was looking at me. I would have been able to feel it with my eyes closed.

"Are you going to ignore me this weekend?"

"That depends?"

"On what?"

"Are you bringing your girlfriend in town with you?"

He winced as I asked the question, but we couldn't pretend like him being with someone else wasn't the truth. He may have been able to forget about her, but I couldn't.

I thought about her every single day.

"I'm not."

A little bit of the tightness in my chest lifted at his words. I saw her on social media, but I didn't think I could handle actually seeing her again. I didn't think my heart would survive really watching him with somebody else.

"Okay." I blinked up at him.

"But you are bringing your boyfriend?" I saw the way his neck tightened and his jaw tensed.

"I am." Even if Ben didn't mean shit to me, I needed him as a buffer. I needed anything that would help protect me from falling right back into Olly.

Because I knew that I would. It would take absolutely no effort for me to forget why he was bad for me. Even talking to him now, it was hard to remember.

"Are you in love with him?"

My gaze snapped back to meet Olly's. "Why would you ask me that?"

"Because I need to know." He adjusted the pillow behind his head roughly. "It drives me crazy to even think about."

"We just started seeing each other, Olly. It's not that serious, and that's not fair."

"Does he make you come like I used to?"

My heart rate spiked as I stared at him. "I'm not going to answer that."

"Because we both already know the truth." He ran his gaze over me, and it didn't matter that he was thousands of miles away. Every inch that his gaze fell on fueled something inside me. "He'll never be able to make you feel like I do."

"You don't make me feel anything anymore, Olly," I answered him and let him hear every bit of anger in my voice.

"We can change that." He ran his fingers through his hair. "It's just you and me here. We can feel whatever we want to feel."

I clamped my thighs together and tried to not let him see how badly his words affected me. "Olly."

"Show me, Frankie." He was watching me so intently. "Show me how you touch yourself."

"This is wrong. We shouldn't be doing this." My hand slid down my belly even as I said the words. I knew I would regret this. It was a mistake, but I felt like a junkie as he spoke. I had been dying for a hit of him.

"Stop worrying about what you should be doing and do what feels right."

I watched him as he adjusted himself in his bed, and I knew that he was touching himself by the way the look on his face shifted. "This feels right. Doesn't it?"

I slid my fingers into my panties, and I was so wet. He wasn't even here, and I was still so wet for him. I ran my finger over my clit and whimpered when a shot of pleasure coursed through me.

"That's it, baby." His voice was so rough. "Imagine that your hand is mine. Think about how desperate I'll be when I finally get to touch you. How hard it will be for me to be easy on you."

My fingers circled my clit, and I sped up as his words fueled me on. I hadn't been this turned on in so long. Not since him.

"How wet are you, Frankie? Tell me."

"I'm so wet." I could barely speak as my orgasm started to build.

"Let me see it. Show me your fingers." His arm was pumping faster and faster.

I pulled my fingers from my pussy with a whimper and showed him. You could see how wet they were, even on the phone screen, and his deep groan told me just how much he liked it.

"Taste it. Tell me if it's as sweet as I remember."

I slid my fingers into my mouth as he watched me, and the way he was looking at me made me feel like I couldn't breathe.

"Fuck." His gaze didn't veer from me as he watched every second of me sucking the wetness from my fingers. "Put them back in your pussy. Show me how badly you wish I was there."

I did so immediately. My body begging for release. I sat up in the bed and slid my panties down my legs. Olly didn't say anything as he watched me, and my hands shook as I propped my phone up on a pillow in front of me and spread my thighs.

"Oh, fuck." Olly jerked forward with a deep groan, and I slid my fingers back through my wetness. I spread it around as he watched, and it felt like the strongest aphrodisiac.

I let my fingers slide into me as I caressed my left breast through my t-shirt with my other hand. "I want to see you too."

Olly rustled around for a moment before he fixed his own phone, and his body came into view. I could still see his face, but I also had a perfect view of his shirtless torso and his cock gripped tightly in his hand.

My fingers sped up as I watched him.

"You are so goddamned beautiful, Frankie. I wish I was the one touching you. I wish I could fuck you with my mouth before I slammed my cock inside of you."

He was pumping his hand harder and faster against his cock, and I followed his lead.

"I want to fuck every inch of you. I would fucking remind you exactly who you belong to."

I whimpered as my orgasm built and built, and I knew that I was so damn close to coming.

"Because you do belong to me, Frankie. Your body, your heart, that perfect little pussy. Every fucking bit of you belongs to me."

I was almost there. So damn close.

"Tell me, baby. Tell me who it all belongs to."

"You." My answer was instant because there wasn't a single question. I had belonged to him for as long as I could remember, and I didn't think there was anything I could do to change that.

Deep down, I was starting to question why I ever wanted to.

"That's fucking right, Frankie. Now come on your fingers while I watch. Show me how badly you wish I was there. Imagine you're coming all over my cock while I fuck every bit of that pleasure from your body."

I tightened my hand around my breast and pushed hard against my clit as my orgasm bombarded me. I screamed his name, and I didn't care that my roommate might hear or the people in the apartment next to us. I had needed that release for so damn long, and my fingers alone had never been enough.

Not like this.

"Fuck." Olly groaned loudly and pointed his cock toward his stomach. I watched as his cum squirted out against his skin and covered his belly.

We sat there in silence for a long time. Both of us trying to catch our breaths and neither of us speaking. I didn't know what to say. I didn't know how to act after what we had just done. We were just watching each other and saying so many things that would never be said out loud.

But even with as good as this felt, I knew it was wrong.

"Are you okay?" His voice startled me.

"Yeah." I nodded and pulled my blanket up to my chest to cover me. I wasn't okay. I didn't know how to be okay. "But I need to get some sleep."

"Yeah." He nodded in agreement. "Me too."

Neither of us hung up, though. We just sat there in silence watching each other breathe, and he was the last thing I saw when my eyes fluttered closed, and I drifted off to sleep.

CHAPTER 6

OLLY

It felt so odd to be back in Clermont Bay after not being here for months. But it felt even odder to come back after the moment Frankie and I had the other night. Especially now that she had stopped answering any calls or texts from me again.

She had answered the other night which was so out of the norm, but now she was back to ignoring me.

I was angry more than anything else. Angry with her. Angry with myself. Pissed that we had let the two of us get this far. I should have never called her the other night. I should have never done something with Frankie that could hurt Jordan regardless of how badly I wanted her.

I was furious that even though I told Jordan that I didn't think things were going to work with us, she was still clinging to me like I was the best thing that ever happened to her. I wasn't.

I was fucking far from it.

And it only made me feel guiltier for the way I felt about Frankie, for the way I fucking craved her.

"So, this is where you rich fucks are from?" Garrett leaned forward between the two front seats and looked around at the houses as we drove down the Clermonts' street.

"It's not nearly as impressive as it looks."

"Yeah." Garrett chuckled. "You all would die if you ever came home with me. I'm pretty sure my entire house could fit in one of your bedrooms."

Carson and I laughed, but Garrett looked dead serious.

"And y'all's parents just let you all have parties at these places?" He was still looking around like he had never seen houses like these before.

"I mean, some do." Carson rubbed at the back of his neck as we pulled into Frankie's driveway. "But Beck's parents are out of town, and his party is going to be really low-key."

I put the car in park and stared ahead at Frankie's. I took a deep breath as my heart raced in my chest. I wasn't sure if I was nervous to face her or if I was just nervous about how she would react to me.

Was she still going to have her boyfriend here? Even after how hard she came for me the other night?

I didn't know what I expected, but part of me hoped that Frankie had told him about me. I hoped that she could forgive me for the mistakes I had made in the past and stopped pushing me away.

I followed Carson as he pushed through the front door, and Garrett followed behind me. The sound of laughter hit us immediately, and I tucked my hands in my pockets.

"Carson!" Allie was off the couch and running in our direction before jumping into his arms. I had become so accustomed to their PDA since living with Carson that I was barely even fazed anymore. Not even when he grabbed her ass and pressed her firmly against him and she giggled.

"How was the flight?" Beck clapped hands with me before pulling me into a hug.

"It was good." I pulled back and nodded to Garrett at my side. "Beck, this is Garrett. Garrett, this is Beck." I pointed to Josie who was curled up on the couch directly behind him. "And that is his girlfriend, Josie." My gaze moved around the room, and I finally spotted Frankie leaning against the doorway that connected the living room and kitchen. "And that's my... that's Frankie."

Shit.

"It's nice to meet you all." Garrett shook hands with Beck, but I couldn't take my eyes off Frankie.

"Hey, Olly." She gently nodded in my direction. Her hair was a little bit longer than I remembered, but it was still the same dark shade that I loved.

"Hi." I took a step toward her but stopped when her gaze flicked away from me quickly. I had no idea what I was doing. I didn't have a fucking clue.

"Are you all ready to party?" Carson called out with his arms wrapped around Allie, and I heard her laugh.

"Don't you fuck up anything in this house, Carson," Josie chastised him as she stood. "I'm not cleaning up after you."

"I wouldn't dream of it."

They were still talking, but I could barely hear a word they said. I was too busy staring at Frankie and picturing the way she had looked on the phone the other night. I had stayed on the line far after she fell asleep, and honestly, that was the part that made me crave her the most.

I had felt desperate to be there with her, to hold her against me while she slept.

My chest ached at the thought. I had to fix this. I had to figure out what the fuck I was doing before I screwed everything up for good.

"Beck, can I talk to you?" As soon as the words passed my lips, there was a loud knock at the door, and Frankie tensed.

"Frankie, is that your boyfriend?" Josie wagged her eyebrows in Frankie's direction.

Frankie looked almost guilty as she looked at me before quickly looking away. "He's not my boyfriend." She moved toward the door. "But please don't fucking embarrass me or I'll never bring a guy back here ever again."

I watched every step she took as she headed toward the door, and Garrett nudged my shoulder with his. I finally pulled my gaze away from her long enough to look over at him.

"Are you okay?" he said low enough for only me to hear.

"Fine." I nodded and clutched my fist at my side.

"You're not pulling it off well."

"Thanks." I watched as Frankie opened the door, but I couldn't see her face or the guy who stood on the other side. It was probably for the best. I didn't know if I could handle watching her looking up at someone else with a smile like she used to look at me.

"So, Garrett, how did you end up with these two?" Josie asked and wrapped her arm around my waist.

I put my arm around her shoulders and pulled her into me. I knew my hold on her was probably too tight, but I held on to her for the support I needed, and she let me.

"Baseball." Garrett shrugged. "I felt bad for their lack of skills on day one and tried to take them under my wings."

"Okay, asshole." I knocked my other hand into his stomach, and he laughed even as Josie nodded her head.

"Olly may not be that good, but he sure does look nice in baseball pants."

I squeezed her harder against me and looked down at her. "Really, Josie? That hurts."

"That was a compliment." She winked at me. "The fact that I even noticed your ass when Beck's was also there is really saying something. It means it's top tier."

"What about mine?" Carson asked as he plopped down on the couch with Allie still against him.

"Ahh." Josie scrunched up her nose. "It's okay."

Everyone chuckled just as Frankie and her guy walked into the room hand in hand, and I knew that Josie was trying her hardest to distract me from them. I loved her for it too.

"Don't worry, Carson." I quickly pulled my gaze away from where his larger hand held hers. "Maybe she at least thinks you're good at the game."

"I think your ass is the best on the field." Allie patted his chest as she looked up at him.

"Her opinion is biased." I rolled my eyes.

"Okay." Carson searched around the room. "Frankie, excluding your brother, for obvious reasons, whose ass is better in baseball pants? Mine or Olly's?"

I couldn't stop the small smile on my lips as I watched her tense at his question. She wasn't going to answer. Her new boyfriend was standing right there beside her, and his brow was scrunched as he took in the question.

"Olly's." Her answer shocked me. "Hands down."

"This is bullshit," Carson grumbled and pulled Allie tighter against him.

"Guys, this is Ben." Frankie interrupted our laughter. "Ben, this is Carson, Allie, Garrett, Josie, and Olly." Her eyes met mine quickly before looking away.

Beck walked up behind Ben and patted his shoulder before taking his hand in his. "It's nice to meet you, Ben. I'm Frankie's brother, Beck."

His reaction to Ben infuriated me, and I held on to Josie tighter. That was all he was going to do? All he was going to say?

"It's nice to meet you too." Ben shook his hand before dropping it, and I knew he had to be feeling awkward in this group. Hell, I would.

"Wow." I laughed to myself. "That's really all Beck has to say?"

Josie smacked my stomach, and I looked down at her. She shook her head as if that was somehow going to make this entire fucking thing better.

"So, what are we doing?" Carson asked. "We drinking, swimming, or heading to the beach?"

"All three." Josie finally let go of me and moved toward Beck. "But we got things ready for a bonfire on the beach, so let's head out there first."

Everyone started heading in different directions. Some outside, some to the kitchen, but I didn't move.

"I'm going to run upstairs and put my suit on." Frankie was talking to Ben, but I was listening to every word. "Why don't you head outside, and I'll meet you out there?"

Ben said something back to her that I couldn't hear, and she smiled just as he walked past her and out of the room. Frankie hesitated, but she didn't say a single word to me or even glance in my direction. She seemed to gather herself before leaving the room and pushing up the stairs.

I stood there and watched every step she took. I couldn't look away from her even if I wanted to, and I knew that it was stupid but everything inside me told me to follow her. I just needed to talk to her alone for one damn second.

Reaching down to get my boardshorts out of my bag, I grabbed them in my hand and headed up the stairs before anyone could question me. I was almost certain that no one was paying attention to me anyway, but I felt so on edge being back here with her.

Going into the guestroom that was adjacent to hers, I quickly changed before tossing my clothes on the bed and heading back out the door. Frankie was still in her room. I could hear her moving around in there. So I leaned against the wall across the hall and waited.

My heart raced and my hands trembled as I lingered by her door, and I swallowed down the shocked breath she let out when she finally opened her door and saw me.

"You scared the shit out of me, Olly." She pressed her hand against her chest and closed the door behind her.

"I'm sorry. I didn't mean to." I bit down on the inside of my lip as I looked at her. She was in a royal blue bikini that showed off every bit of her curves, but that wasn't where I was looking. It was the sadness in her eyes that she hid as she quickly looked away from me that took my breath away. "I just wanted to make sure you were okay."

She laughed and pushed her long hair out of her face with fumbling fingers. "I am perfectly fine, Olly. I've been perfectly fine without you for quite some time, but thank you for checking." Her voice was so cold.

She went to move past me, but I reached out and touched my fingers against hers and she stopped.

"I didn't mean it like that." I shook my head as my heart raced in my chest. "I know that you are more than capable of taking care of yourself. I just meant after the other night. I tried to call you again, but you've been ignoring me."

"That's because the other night shouldn't have happened." She looked at me before looking back down the hall, but there was no one up here except me and her. "It was a slip of judgment on both of our parts."

"Was it?" I cocked my head to the side and studied her. We both knew what we were doing the other night when I called her, but the thought of her regretting it, of her regretting me, felt so heavy in my chest.

"It was." She searched my face, and for a moment, I thought she was going to step forward and kiss me. I could see the want in her eyes. The tremble of her fingers against mine. The desire to do just that, but she stopped herself. "I have managed to be fine without you for so long now, and then you call me and..."

She shook her head, but I was dying for her to finish that sentence.

"And what?"

"And I fall back into your bullshit like you aren't the guy who broke my heart."

My heart felt like it was going to beat out of my chest as I stepped forward and tried to close the gap between us. Shame slammed into me as I let her words sink in. "You know that I never meant to. That was never what I wanted."

"I know." She shrugged her shoulders. "But it doesn't change the fact that you did. I know what happened between us was messy and things were hard, but you still didn't choose me. I loved you and you didn't choose me."

"Is that what you want me to do?" I could feel my panic rising with each second. "I can go downstairs right now and tell Beck that this is what I want. I already told Jordan that this is what I want."

There was shock in her eyes at my confession, but she quickly hid it. "Don't do that. Don't ruin your relationship with a girl you like for something that isn't even real anymore."

"It is real."

"No." She held up her hand and pressed it against my chest as if that would keep me away from her. "It's not. I'm not sure if it ever was."

"You know that's a lie."

"What I know is that I have a guy downstairs who is waiting on me. A guy who isn't worried about who is going to see me with him." There was so much pain in her eyes, and I was desperate to take it away. I wished I could take back so many things that I couldn't.

I gripped the back of her head in my hand and pulled her closer to me. Her hand was pressed tightly between us, but she didn't fight it.

"I never wanted to hurt you." I ran my nose along her jaw and drank in the smell and feel of her. God, I had missed this so much. I missed her.

I missed the way she sounded when she breathed against me. The way she looked up at me with her brown eyes begging me for more. She still had the same soft hint of coconut that made me crave summer, and my fingers burned where my skin connected with hers.

I never wanted to go so long without touching her again.

"I never want to hurt you again." I ran my lips over hers gently, and she took a shuttering breath before the tiniest whimper passed through her lips. "I never want to give you up."

I pressed my lips against hers timidly because I had no idea what she was thinking. Despite what happened between us on the phone the other night, her actions and her words were so different from one another.

But she closed the kiss before I could gather the courage, and she gripped her hand in my shirt and held me against her. I couldn't stop after that. I could barely think.

I kissed her with everything I had. I put every bit of want and need and pure fucking desperation into that kiss, and she matched my need with every move. We slammed into the wall, my arm taking the brunt of the hit, and she scrambled to get her arms out from between us and around my neck.

She held me to her as she kissed me, and I sucked her bottom lip into my mouth just as she raised her legs and wrapped them around my hips. I pressed harder against her, the weight of my body holding hers up, and I knew she could feel how badly I wanted her.

Every part of me trembled with a need to touch her, taste her, claim her.

There was barely any material between us, and I could have easily slipped her bikini to the side and touched every inch of her if I wanted to. And trust me, I fucking wanted to.

But I didn't want her to think that this was about sex for me. It wasn't. Did I crave her body more than I had ever wanted anything else in my life? Absolutely. But the deep ache in my chest had nothing to do with her body.

I wanted her. Her mind, her kindness, her sass. I missed every damn bit of her.

I softened my kiss against her lips before moving along her cheek. I kissed her slowly, deliberately, as I moved down and around her jaw.

Frankie tightened her legs around my waist and ground against me. It was so overwhelming, the feel of her, the taste of her on my tongue. Every touch making me yearn for more and more.

"I need you to do something." She tugged on my neck and tried to pull me back to her mouth as she rode my hips with hers. I was so hard against her, and I knew that my cock was hitting places on her body that made her feel as wild with lust as I did.

"I am doing something." I ran my nose along her jaw before pressing a soft kiss beneath her ear.

"No. I need you to move. To touch me."

"And I need you to go down there and send your boyfriend home." The moment the words passed my lips, I knew that was the wrong thing to say. Frankie's body stiffened beneath mine, and her fingers fell from my neck.

I wrapped my hands around her thighs so she wouldn't push away from me completely, but it was no use.

"Let me go."

"No." I shook my head against her neck. "I'm not ready to give you up."

"It doesn't matter." She pushed against my chest, and I finally let her feet drop to the floor. "I'm not yours to give up, Olly. I am not yours at all."

Anger flooded me even though I knew it shouldn't. What she was saying was the truth, but that didn't make it any easier to hear.

"You felt like mine when you were just begging me."

Her shocked inhale stole my own breath, and I wished I could take back my words. I wished I could take back everything I had ever said that hurt her, but somehow, I kept doing it again and again.

"Don't get a big head because I miss your cock, Olly." She pushed against my chest, and I took a step back. I knew she meant for her words to hurt me, but they didn't. She could say what she wanted, but I knew she missed me.

If she didn't, she would have never answered the phone the other night. She would have never let things go this far.

"That's the only thing you miss about me?"

"Right now?" She straightened out her hair and her bikini. "Absolutely."

She headed toward the stairs, and I followed right behind her before she turned back to me with her finger pointed in my face. "Do not follow me down the stairs and make Ben think something is going on between us. You remember how to sneak around? You were very good at it at one point."

"But there is something going on between us."

"No. There's not. This..." She motioned back and forth between us. "Is never going to happen again." Then she marched down the stairs to the guy who was waiting for her, and I had no choice but to watch her go.

CHAPTER 7
FRANKIE

What the fuck was I doing?

That was the thought that continuously ran through my mind as I stormed down the stairs and out the back door. Ben was standing next to my brother and already had a beer in his hand.

He smiled when he saw me walk out the door, and I was flooded with guilt. I barely knew this guy, but already I was doing things that I knew he didn't deserve.

Because of Olly.

Every decision I made over the last year was always with Olly in the back of my mind.

And I hated it.

"Hey." Ben reached his hand out in my direction, and I let him wrap it around my waist as he pulled me into him. His gaze roamed over my body, and I wondered if he could see Olly's touch on my skin.

Had he left a mark on my skin like he had everything else?

Ben and I had only hung out one other time since we

met at the bar, and even though it had been enjoyable, I still felt awkward.

I barely even knew the guy, and I had been an idiot for inviting him here.

"Hi." I pushed my hair out of my face and looked up at him. Ben was handsome, but my first thought when I saw his smile was that he wasn't Olly.

But I knew I had to get used to that. I had to accept that the guy I ended up with wouldn't be the same guy who I loved with a desperation that wasn't healthy.

Nothing about the two of us ever was.

But that didn't mean I loved him any less.

It just meant that I had to figure out how to love someone differently.

"Is everyone being nice to you?" I looked over at Beck, and he had the nerve to actually wink at me. The asshole.

"Of course." Ben laughed and pulled me closer to him. I tensed the smallest bit as he leaned closer to me and spoke where only I could hear him. "You look amazing."

I smiled and tried to let his words affect me. I begged them to do anything. "Thank you." I looked away from him when nothing came. "Let's head down to the beach."

I gripped his hand in mine and pulled him behind me just as the back door opened. I knew it was Olly, but I didn't dare look back. I knew I wouldn't be able to pull this off if I met his eyes for even a second.

I wasn't going to be able to pretend like I wasn't falling apart from seeing him.

I had asked him to touch me up there. Practically begged him to give me something that I knew I shouldn't have, and I was so damn embarrassed by how weak he made me.

I wasn't the same girl that loved Olly back then. I had

changed, but when he touched me, I felt like I was right back where we started. It was hard to remember that he didn't choose me. It was impossible to wrap my head around the idea that he wasn't good for me.

Sometimes I wished I could forget about him altogether, but the thought of living in a world where the two of us didn't connect in some way made my chest ache so badly it stole my breath.

As desperately as I wanted to forget Olly, I craved the idea of him never walking away again.

And that kind of want was treacherous. I would follow that desire until it led to nothing but misery. I knew that with certainty.

Olly had hurt me before, and he would hurt me again.

I was the only one who could protect myself from him, and I wasn't sure if I was capable.

"This beach is so nice." Ben looked around as we pushed through the sand, and I realized how tightly I was clinging to his hand.

"It is." I nodded. "It's my favorite place in the world."

"I can see why." He smiled down at me, and he looked so genuinely happy to be here with me.

"So, Ben? Where did you and Frankie meet?" I looked over my shoulder at Olly as he sat down in the sand.

"We met at this little bar right down the street from our university." Ben chuckled before taking a seat near the fire. I followed him and pressed against his side as the warm sand pressed against my legs. "I knocked her tequila all over her."

"Tequila?" Olly cocked his head slightly. "Frankie, how is a nineteen-year-old managing to get tequila at a bar?"

I looked him straight in the eyes as I answered him. "You

know what they say. It's all about who you know and who you blow."

Ben jerked back the smallest bit as if he was shocked by my answer, but I didn't care. I wasn't looking at him. I was too busy watching the way Olly's eyes darkened and his fist clenched in the sand.

"Okay." He nodded his head with a bitter smile on his lips. "Have you two been dating long?"

He looked back toward Ben.

"Uh, no." I heard Ben chuckle beside me. "We actually just met recently."

"Wow. She must really like you to bring you home to meet everyone so quickly."

"I hope so." Ben ran his hand down my bare back, and I tried not to let Olly see me flinch at his touch. "What about you?" Ben nodded in Olly's direction. "Do you have a girl around here?"

"You could say that."

My eyes slammed into Olly's, and my anger rose. "Olly doesn't live here anymore. He moved to California, and he definitely has a girlfriend there."

"Oh. That's cool." Ben nodded. "I've always wanted to go to Cali."

"It was kind of a letdown for me." I pulled my attention away from Olly to look back at Ben. "I expected a lot more out of it, honestly."

"But she really didn't give it a chance."

"Yes. I did," I snapped back at him, and narrow my eyes. "I gave it more chances than it deserved."

"Okay." Carson clapped his hands together, and my attention was drawn to where he stood. Beck and Josie were walking up behind him, and Beck was carrying a large white cooler. "Anyone want to go for a swim?"

"Me." I pushed off the sand before dusting it off my legs. I needed to get away from Olly before I said something that I was going to regret.

He knew what he was doing. He was trying to get a reaction out of me in front of Ben, and I was falling right into his trap.

"Want to get in?" I held my hand out to Ben, and he quickly took it. He smiled as he stood and pulled his t-shirt over his head.

I pulled him toward me, right where Olly could see, and I smiled up at him like I had never been happier to be with anyone else. I smiled up at him like I knew I usually looked at Olly.

"Let's go." I stepped backward with his hand in mine, and my gaze only flashed to Olly's for a second. The anger I saw there should have stopped me. I should have second-guessed every decision I was making, but I didn't.

I just pulled Ben into the ocean, and I told myself that I didn't care what Olly thought.

It was just another lie, and it was one that I told myself for the rest of the night.

CHAPTER 8
FRANKIE

"Did your boyfriend finally leave?"

I spun around to find Olly standing behind me, and I hated how that one damn look did so many things to me. "Don't be a dick, Olly. It doesn't suit you." I walked back through the dark foyer and headed toward the kitchen.

"What would you prefer I be, Frankie?" He followed every step I took, and I could feel the heat of him against my back.

"Honestly? I don't know." I shook my head and turned just in time to press my hand against his chest to stop him from coming any closer. I knew that Josie had already taken my drunk brother to bed, but everyone else was still out by the pool, and this wasn't a conversation that I wanted anyone else to walk in on. "But we're not talking about this right now."

"Yes. We are." He pushed even closer to me, and I took a step back until my back pressed into the cold granite of the countertops. "If I don't force you to have this conversation now, then you'll just ignore me and it'll never happen."

"Maybe that's for the best." I looked up at him, and it was so hard to breathe with the way he was looking down at me. His dark eyes were heady and filled with something that went so much further than want.

"We both know that isn't true." His bare chest was pressed against my hand and his brown hair was falling into his face. He was so damn handsome that it hurt. "Tell me you won't have regrets when I leave."

"I always have regrets when it comes to you."

He winced, and I saw the pain slice across his features.

"That's not what I meant."

"Yeah." He nodded. "It is." He lifted his hand and gently pushed some hair out of my face. I held my breath as he did so. He was doing nothing but touching my fucking hair, but I still felt more in that one simple move than I had all day with Ben. "But I don't blame you."

"You don't get to do this, Olly." I tried my hardest to harden my heart as I spoke. "You don't get to act like you aren't the one who chose this. What we are is because of you."

"You act like I could have just changed everything. Like I could have made everyone else disappear."

I swallowed deep and hard. "You could have, but you didn't. You chose them over me."

"That's not fair." His eyes searched mine, and I could have sworn he moved even closer to me.

"I didn't say it was, but none of this has been fair to me."

"What did you want me to do, Frankie? I would have lost everyone."

"Except me." I looked down at his chest, and I told myself to school my features, to guard my heart. "You wouldn't have lost me."

"What can I do, Frankie? Tell me what to do."

I shook my head because I didn't know what to tell him. I didn't see a way we could ever make something work between us and not end up hurting each other.

"Do you want me to act like Ben? Would you prefer that I didn't know a single fucking thing about you or what you like? Would that make you want me more?"

My gaze snapped back up to him, and my heart raced as anger flooded me at his words.

"You don't know a damn thing about Ben or me."

"Yes, I do." He gripped my chin in his hand and held me in place so I had no choice but to look at him. "I know that you don't fucking want him. I know that he doesn't make your body feel a single fucking thing like it does when I touch you."

He was right, but he was also wrong. I hadn't even given Ben the opportunity. I hadn't given anyone the chance, but I wouldn't allow him to have that knowledge.

Instead, I straightened my spine and looked him directly in the eyes. "No one has ever fucked me the way Ben does. He makes me come harder than you could dream."

There was a flash in his eyes that made my knees feel like they were going to buckle. One simple lie fueled him, and the way he was looking at me told me that he was going to prove me wrong. He was determined to make sure that I didn't forget it.

"Don't fucking test me, Frankie." His grip on my chin was almost painful. "I will bend you over this counter right now and fuck you until you remember exactly what it feels like to be mine. I will make you forget that anyone but me has ever touched your perfect fucking body."

I didn't dare budge. I tried my damnedest not to let him

see how much I was affected by his words, but I couldn't stop myself from pressing my thighs together to calm the ache there. "I have a boyfriend, Olly."

"And I don't give a fuck about him." He lowered until his gaze was directly in mine. "You are mine."

I sucked in a sharp breath as my chest heaved.

"I'm not."

"Yes. You fucking are." He didn't give me a warning or any time to react as he jerked me forward and slammed his mouth against mine. His mouth was harsh and punishing, and I could hardly breathe as his lips bruised mine.

His other hand gripped my bare thigh, and he lifted me in one swift movement and planted my ass on the counter. I looked toward the window, but he tugged me back to his mouth before I could really worry about who was outside watching us.

He made me forget everything that wasn't the two of us at that moment, and he made it hard to remember why this wasn't a good idea.

He kissed down my jaw, his teeth dragging over my sensitive skin before he eased over it with his tongue, and my body trembled against him. He moved along my neck, worshipping every damn spot he passed, and God, I had missed this. I had missed him so damn much.

"Tell me you want this," he whispered against my ear before biting down gently against my earlobe.

"I want it." My response was instant because I didn't stand a chance at hiding it from him.

He leaned back the slightest bit and ran his gaze down my bikini-clad body. My thighs shook at his sides, and he stared up at me as he leaned down and pressed a kiss along my breastbone. He wasted no time as he pulled my top down and exposed my breasts to him.

"You are so fucking beautiful," he murmured against my skin before running his tongue against my nipple. He pulled it in his mouth as his hand lifted and he molded my other breast in his fingers. "Are you fucking wet for me, Frankie?"

I moaned at his question and the way his mouth was moving against my breast, but that answer wasn't good enough for him.

"Tell me how wet you are. Tell me if you've ever been this wet for anyone other than me," he growled against my skin, and even though I wanted to lie to him, I knew that I couldn't.

"You know I haven't." I shook my head.

He dropped his hand and slid it against my bikini bottoms, and I knew that he could feel the moisture leaking through them.

"So fucking wet," he moaned before lifting his head and bringing his mouth back to mine.

He pushed my bathing suit aside and slid his fingers against my pussy, and I tensed at the contact. If he noticed, he didn't let on. He simply pushed his fingers through every inch of me as if he couldn't believe that he was touching me again. He was committing my body to memory, and I was getting wetter and wetter with every second that passed.

"Olly." I reached out for him, but he grabbed my leg in his hand and brought my foot up until it was pressed against the counter in front of me.

He stared at me before pressing his hand against my chest and pushing me flat against the counter. "I'm going to die if I don't taste this pussy," he groaned.

"Oh God." My back bowed off the counter as he lowered his head, and anticipation thrummed through my body.

This was more than just sex. I wanted to deny him, but I felt desperate for him to touch me. I felt like I was going to go insane if I wasn't able to connect with him in a way that no one else could give me.

This was ours. It belonged to no one else besides us, and even though I knew he had been with others, I tried to convince myself that it had never been like this for him with anyone else.

Only me and him.

He pulled my bottoms down my hips, and I lifted my ass off the counter to allow him to pull them down my legs. I was so exposed in front of him, but I didn't feel a bit of timidness. My body was his to do what he wanted with, and I knew that I would probably never feel so comfortable with anyone else in my life.

Olly had hurt me, but he had also healed me, and part of me would always belong to him.

"Fuck." He pressed his rough hands against the inside of my knees and spread my legs as far as they would go as he stared down at my pussy. He dropped his head before I could manage to say a word, and he wasted no time running his tongue through my slit.

"Oh my God." I pushed my fingers into his hair and slammed my head back against the counter.

His tongue hit my clit, and he didn't stop. He flicked his tongue there gently before moving it faster and harder, and my legs trembled at his sides as he sucked the small bud into his mouth.

Anything I had ever done with my own hand had never compared to this. Nothing compared to him.

"God, you taste so fucking good." His teeth ran over my clit, and I shot up as a scream clawed up my throat. "It's just like I remember. It's the exact taste I imagine when my cock is in my hand."

His words were as intoxicating as his mouth, and my stomach tightened as my orgasm raced through me at an embarrassingly fast speed. I was so damn close.

He pushed two fingers inside of me as he continued to work me with his mouth, and I just needed one more touch. One more curl of his fingers or caress of his tongue and I would be there. But he let off, and I jerked forward to look at him.

He was staring directly at me, his mouth hovering over my soaking wet pussy, and his fingers still inside me. "Tell me that you're mine. Tell me who this pussy belongs to."

"You're insane." I could barely breathe as I answered him. I just needed him to move, to do something. Anything that would let me come.

He lowered his head as he stared up at me and blew a gentle breath against my clit. I jerked forward, my body forcing his fingers harder inside me, and I could feel my orgasm right on the brink.

"Tell me, Frankie."

"Olly, I am so fucking close, please."

"I know." He pressed a soft kiss against my clit, and the feeling was far more intense than it should have been.

His fingers moved faster inside of me, and he curled them up until they were touching that spot inside of me that I could never seem to hit on my own. His tongue lapped against me, right where his fingers were sliding in and out, before he moved back to my clit and worked it with his tongue.

I couldn't sit still as I moved against him and rode his face. My fingers were still laced in his hair, and I held him against me as I silently begged him.

This time he didn't lift his head as he spoke. He murmured his words against my pussy, but they were crystal fucking clear. "Whose pussy is this, Frankie?"

I tightened my hands in his hair as I tried to resist him, but it was no use. We both knew the answer already, and it didn't matter how much I tried to prove him otherwise.

"Yours," I finally answered him. "It's always been yours."

He growled against me and sucked my clit into his mouth, and I came with a scream. I covered my mouth with my hand to try to muffle the sound, but it was no use.

Olly pulled me from the counter and dropped my feet to the ground in a rush as he spun me away from him. I could feel his hard cock pressing against my ass as he kissed the back of my neck and ran his tongue down my spine.

He pressed his hand there, and I allowed him to push me until my upper body was pressed back against the counter and my ass was on display in front of him. I could hear him fumbling with his shorts before I felt the smooth skin of his cock against my ass. He ran it up and down, hitting my pussy before pushing back through my ass cheeks, and my body was still thrumming from my orgasm.

"Fuck, I don't have a condom," he cursed, and I looked over my shoulder at him. He looked as crazed as I felt, so lost in our lust for one another that nothing else seemed to matter.

"It's okay." I swallowed hard. "I'm on birth control."

His gaze met mine, and I knew this really wasn't a conversation either one of us wanted to have. He thought I was on birth control for Ben.

"I'm clean." He ran his hand gently over my lower back. "You're the only person I've ever not used a condom with."

I closed my eyes at his confession. That should have made me happy, but all I could think about was the fact that he had used a condom with someone else. With her. While I could barely manage to kiss another guy without thoughts of him flooding me, he had been fucking someone else just fine.

"I trust you," I said the words before looking away. Even though they hurt, those words were still the truth. I still trusted him more than I had ever trusted anyone else even after everything.

"God," he groaned. "You saying that fucks with my head. It's the sexiest fucking thing."

He ran his cock against me again, and I whimpered when he pressed it against my sensitive clit. He pulled away from me, and I looked back over my shoulder again just before he dropped down behind me. His fingers dug into my ass and he spread me apart just before his mouth met my pussy again.

He rolled his tongue against me, and I lifted on my tiptoes as I chased the feeling. He bit down just where my ass cheek met my leg, and I squirmed against him.

"You are so fucking ready for me."

I nodded frantically as I pushed my ass against him. I felt desperate to feel him inside me.

He stood again and I felt the head of him push against my entrance. He pushed inside of me, slowly at first, before slamming in hard to the hilt, and I grasped for something to hold on to as my chest slid against the granite.

Olly reached forward and grabbed my hands in his, and he continued to slide in and out of me as he brought my hands together at the small of my back and held them in one of his. My back arched and my nipples pressed harshly into the cold granite.

Olly moved his other hand back to my ass, and I tensed as he pulled me apart and watched where his body slid into mine. "You are so fucking perfect, Frankie. So fucking perfect for me."

I tried my hardest to block out his words, but every last one bombarded me and made me feel far more than I wanted to. He made me feel things that I had been grappling to try to forget.

He fucked me hard yet slowly, as if he couldn't control himself but was trying to savor me all at once, and every single thrust seemed to steal some part of me that I didn't give him permission to take.

He pulled out of me, and I was just about to ask what he was doing when he dropped my hands and lifted me back against him. I stood on shaky legs and looked over my shoulder just as he scooped an arm beneath my legs and lifted me into his arms.

"What are you doing?" I clung to his shoulders and looked around as he moved out of the kitchen, leaving both of our bathing suit bottoms on the floor. "Someone is going to see those."

"I don't give a fuck what anyone sees." He headed toward the stairs and carried me up them as if I weighed nothing.

"Where are we going?"

"I've been fantasizing about fucking you in your fucking bed for years."

I pressed my thighs together as we hit the top of the stairs and Olly moved down the dark hallway. "Technically, this isn't really my bed anymore."

He looked down at me with his dark eyes, and I was almost certain that he could eat me whole. "Then we'll start here and then I'll take you to your apartment and fuck you on every possible surface I can find there."

"Maybe I don't want you there."

He fumbled with my door handle before walking through and kicking the door shut behind us. "We both know you do." He dropped me down on my bed before crawling up between my thighs. I moved higher in the bed until my head hit the pillow, and he followed my every move.

He caught my jaw in his hand and he kissed me as his body pressed down against mine. I could feel every inch of him like this, and my fingers grazed down his sides as his tongue rolled against mine.

"I want to see your eyes when you come again," he murmured against my lips before pushing up onto his knees between my thighs. "I want you to be looking directly at me when I remind you what you're missing."

"You don't have to remind me, Olly." I shook my head just as he pushed inside me. "Even when you're a thousand miles away from me, and I miss you every damn second. I've never stopped."

He slammed into me then as if he could no longer control himself, and his mouth ran over my body. He kissed my breasts, my chest, my neck, anything he could get a hold of as he fucked me, and it was all so overwhelming.

My chest ached and my pussy clenched around him over and over. I didn't know what to do or say or feel. All I knew was that I wanted more. More of him, more of this, more than what I was allowed to take.

"Fuck." He leaned back on his knees and gathered my right thigh against him. He pressed his hand down against my shin, spreading me completely open for him, and his thumb pushed down against my clit.

I surged forward, my body so lost in everything he was doing, and when his next words hit me, I knew that I wouldn't be able to handle them.

"I love you, Frankie. God. I fucking love you so much."

I clamped my eyes closed and my hips moved faster. Please, please, please. I needed my orgasm to distract me. I needed it to surge through my body and ease the pain that was clawing at me with every passing second.

"I've never stopped loving you." He slammed into me with so much force that I was forced up higher in the bed, and my pussy clenched around him as I could feel my orgasm building and building. I only needed a little bit more.

"I'll never stop." He slapped his hand down against my pussy, his fingers hitting my clit just before he applied pressure to my lower stomach, and I came so hard that I didn't stand a chance of replying to him.

I loved him. We both knew that I did, but I couldn't risk saying it out loud. Saying it made things real.

It made things dangerous.

"Oh, fuck." I slammed my hand down against my mouth, but he quickly pulled it away and replaced it with his mouth against mine. He kissed me hard and brutally as he pumped into me two more times. Then I felt him come inside me with a harsh jerk that sent aftershocks through my body.

With each ebb and flow of pleasure that coursed through me came an equally powerful wave of anguish. This was exactly why Olly and I could never be. I knew that what we had just done was wrong. I knew he was bad for me, but it didn't matter.

I was weak when it came to him, and I hated how vulnerable it made me feel. He could hurt me, break me so easily. All it would take is one decision from him.

Right now, all he could see was how badly he wanted me, but that could change so easily. And I wouldn't survive Olly not choosing me again.

I couldn't allow him to be everything to me when he could rip it away effortlessly.

CHAPTER 9
OLLY

I blinked my eyes open and groaned as the sunlight flooded the room. My right arm was asleep, and I looked down to find Frankie fast asleep against my chest.

Frankie.

Fuck.

I didn't regret what happened last night for a second, but I did regret that I hadn't done things differently. This wasn't what I wanted. I didn't want her to think that I was here to fuck her then walk away. That was so fucking far from the truth.

But I did this all wrong.

I slowly pulled my arm out from under her head, and she shifted onto her back before burying her head back into her pillow. She looked so damn peaceful and beautiful, and I pressed a gentle kiss against her shoulder before slowly climbing out of her bed.

I was naked. Butt-ass naked, and it hit me at that moment that I had left both of our bathing suits laying on the floor in the kitchen.

If Beck hadn't wanted to kill me before, he definitely would when he saw that. Because despite how I felt about everything, Beck did deserve to know the truth. His opinion no longer mattered. Not really. It wouldn't stop me from loving his sister.

But as angry as I was at him for every part he played in this, I needed to tell him the truth. I should have done it a long time ago. Even if it didn't make a difference for Frankie, even if she still didn't want this, she deserved more than I was giving her.

I hadn't thought telling Beck mattered when there was nothing really going on between us, but I was wrong.

I was so fucking wrong.

I grabbed a towel from the bathroom and wrapped it around my waist before I eased out her door and closed it softly behind me.

I didn't hear any sound through the house, but that didn't really mean anything. This house was massive, and every single person could be awake downstairs and I wouldn't know it.

I tightened my hand around my towel and eased down the stairs. It wasn't until I pushed through the kitchen threshold that I finally heard someone clear their throat, and I looked to my right to find Carson and Garrett sitting at the kitchen table with shit-eating grins on their faces.

Carson held my boardshorts from the tip of his finger, and he cocked his head to the side when he saw me notice them. "It would appear that you had an interesting night."

I made my way over to him and jerked my shorts off his hand before tugging them up my legs.

"Where are Frankie's bottoms?"

"How am I supposed to know?" He put his hand against

his chest as Garrett chuckled. "I'm not the one who removed them from her body and threw them halfway across the kitchen."

"Are you done?" I looked back and forth between them.

"Not even close." Carson leaned forward and the smile dropped from his face. "What the fuck are you thinking?"

"I don't know."

"That's fucking clear." He shook his head. "Do you remember why you broke things off with her in the first place? Your best friend, and that best friend is currently asleep right out there." He pointed to the pool house. "What would you have done if he had walked in on you fucking his sister?"

I shrugged my shoulders even as my heart raced. "I'm not sure I care anymore."

"Yes. You do."

"Not as much as I care about her."

They were both silent for a minute after that, and I knew that Carson realized how serious I was. Leaving for California put a lot of things in perspective for me. Beck was one of my best friends, and he always would be, but I couldn't live without Frankie.

It was that simple.

And it was something I hadn't realized when I should have.

"Oh my God." Beck pushed through the back door, and all three of us swung our heads in his direction. "Who the fuck let me drink that much?"

"That would be you." Carson laughed and stood from the table. "Trying to take a drink out of your hand was like trying to wrestle a bear."

Beck rolled his eyes and pulled an energy drink out of

the refrigerator before hopping up on the counter. On the same damn counter where I had fucked his sister the night before. "Where are Frankie and Allie?"

"Still sleeping." Carson dropped his bowl in the sink before turning back to me and making eyes at me. "Josie too?"

"Yeah." Beck nodded. "She wasn't budging. That girl can sleep like the dead."

"So what do you all want to do until they get up?" Carson looked between all of us, and I ran my fingers over the back of my neck as my heart raced.

"Actually, Beck, I need to talk to you first."

"Okay." Beck looked back and forth between me and Carson, and I actually felt a little bad for Garrett. He barely knew any of these damn people, and here I was putting him right in the middle of the drama. "Do Carson and Garrett need to leave for this conversation?"

"Probably." I nodded, but Carson shook his head.

"No. I think it's best I stay so you two don't kill each other."

"Ah." Beck set his drink down on the counter and crossed his arms. "So this is going to be that kind of conversation."

"It's about Frankie."

"What about her?" His shoulders stiffened and his jaw clenched.

"I just feel like you should know that I'm in love with her." I laid it out there because I was so tired of tiptoeing around the truth. "I've been in love with her, and we should have had this conversation a long fucking time ago."

Beck didn't say anything for a long moment. He just studied me as if he was trying to figure out whether I was being honest or not. I hated that I had made him question my word, but I hated everything I had done to Frankie so much more.

"She has a boyfriend, and you have a girlfriend."

"Jordan knows how I feel about Frankie. I told her everything before we left California. She knows that I'm here to see her, and she knows that I'm still in love with her."

"And what about Ben?" He narrowed his eyes at me, and I clenched my fist in my lap.

"I really don't give a fuck about Ben." I shrugged at him because I honestly didn't know what else to say. "I am in love with your sister."

"You two have barely talked since you've been gone."

"It doesn't matter. I've been in love with her since before I left." I stood because I felt like I was going to go crazy sitting there. "That shit doesn't just go away."

"And what about Frankie?"

"What about her?"

"She was here with another guy last night. A guy who looks like he's really good for her."

"I'm not sure why you feel that I'm not fucking good for her. I am not Lucas."

He winced and was quiet for a long moment.

"I know you're not." He ran his hands through her hair.

"I gave her up for you." I pointed at him as I could feel my anger rising. "I hurt her because you refused to see how good I was for her, and now, I don't know that she'll ever want this again."

"You're right." He looked up at me with guilt. He ran his hand over his hair, and I could see his mind racing. "Did you sleep with her again?"

I stared at him, and it was clear that he knew the answer

before I even opened my mouth. "Do you really want to know the answer to that?"

"I wouldn't have fucking asked you if I didn't."

"Then yes." I nodded and stood my ground. "I slept with her last night."

Something passed over his face, but I couldn't tell what he was thinking. Even though I knew he had the right to be angry since I betrayed his trust after I promised him I wouldn't, I didn't fear his anger like I did before. I didn't need his approval.

"Before you say anything, though, I have kept my distance from her for a long time because that was what you wanted. Not me and not her. And that's not fucking fair. I want to be with Frankie, and I will be whether you are okay with it or not."

"You all cannot be serious." I spun around at the sound of Frankie's voice to see her standing in the doorway watching us.

"Frankie." I took a step toward her and reached out my hand before I thought better of it. She was wearing an over-sized t-shirt and her hair was piled on top of her head, and even though she looked like she was ready to kill us all, she was so damn beautiful.

"Don't." She shook her head and looked away from me. "You all have got to be out of your damn minds."

She took a step into the kitchen and moved toward the fridge without saying another word. All of us were watching her as she grabbed a bottle of water, and we all seemed to jump at the exact same time when she slammed the refrigerator door closed and spun back toward us.

"When are you going to grow the fuck up?" She pointed her finger at her brother, and he stiffened.

"What the hell did I do?" He put his hand against his chest as he scrunched his brows.

"You." She hesitated and gripped her water bottle in her hands. "You think that you can still make decisions for me even though I'm a grown-ass woman. Do you think it's up to you whether or not I fuck Olly? I didn't see you giving Ben the same fifth degree. I don't see you walking around my college campus questioning every guy I've ever met."

"That's different, and you know it."

"No. It's not." She took a step closer to him and the bottle groaned under her grip. Her knuckles were turning white as her frustration seeped out of her. "I get that one of your friends betrayed you, but Olly is not Lucas. Stop fucking treating him like he was the one who assaulted me. I have gotten past what happened, Beck. I have been to countless therapy sessions. I have healed. It is time you do the same."

I was so proud of her for standing up to him, and the urge to tell her so was almost overwhelming, but then she turned her angry gaze toward me. "And you." She moved in my direction and pushed her hand against my chest. "You don't get to decide what happens between us. Just because I had a lapse of judgment and slept with you again, doesn't mean that you need to run to my brother and make some stupid proclamation of love. It was sex, Olly."

My chest ached as she said the words, and I clenched my jaw so tightly that I feared it might snap. I knew that what happened between us last night wasn't just sex. It never had been. "We both know that isn't true."

"No." She pushed against my chest even harder as I took a step back. "All you know is what you think, Olly. And you think you know what I want, but you don't." She looked around the room. "None of you do. None of you stop for a damn second to think about what anyone wants but you."

I reached out for her, and when I held her hand in mine, she looked down at it. I could tell that what she was saying was hurting her as much as it was me, and I wanted her to stop. I wanted both of us to stop doing things that meant we couldn't be together.

"Tell me what you want me to do."

She shook her head and bit down on her bottom lip before glancing back up at me. There was so much sadness in her eyes, but it was clouded by her strength. "There is nothing for you to do, Olly. You made your decision about us before, and you don't get to just change your mind because you finally figured out what you want." She took a deep breath and pulled her hand from mine. "You don't get to want me because you suddenly decided that I'm good enough."

"There's the birthday boy!" I heard Josie's voice, but I didn't turn around to look at her. I wasn't sure if anyone did. "Oh shit. What happened?"

"Nothing." Frankie smiled and looked over at her friend. "What are we doing today to celebrate?"

"Frankie," I said her name so softly that I wasn't sure she would hear me, but she simply shook her head.

"I thought we might head down to the boardwalk and get tacos," Josie said hesitantly.

"I'm down." Frankie opened her bottle of water and took a long drink. "I just need to get dressed first."

"I'll stay back." I took a step back from Frankie and finally looked over at Josie. What the fuck was I doing? "I may head back to school early."

"What?" Frankie jerked her gaze back to me. "You're not doing that."

I didn't answer her. Instead, I turned back toward Beck. "Your board still in the garage? I think I want to catch some waves."

"Yeah." He nodded, and I could tell he was hesitant as he looked back and forth between me and his sister.

"Cool." I didn't wait for any of them to respond again. I simply pushed through the kitchen and out to the garage, and I didn't stop until I had Beck's surfboard in my hand and the sand under my feet.

The beach was calm and empty this early in the day, but the ocean softly crashed against the sand with deep waves. It was perfect.

I needed to clear my damn head because I felt more confused than ever.

I waded out into the ocean and the warm water lapped at my shins. Already I could feel a bit of tension leave my body as a familiar rush filled me.

I pushed out farther and laid the board against the surface. Climbing on top, I let my chest fall against the hard board and started paddling out. I didn't stop until I felt a slight burn in my arms.

Sitting up, I let my legs dangle off the sides into the water, and I pushed my hair out of my face. I took a deep breath and tried to let it ground me.

This was one of the biggest things I missed while I was in California. Of course, there were beaches and the ocean there, but it wasn't the same. It didn't feel like home. It didn't give me a feeling in my gut that made me ache for something I couldn't quite grasp.

The sun was bright and high in the sky, and I lifted my

face and soaked in the rays. It made me feel like I could breathe just a bit easier than before.

And I needed all the help I could get because Frankie didn't want to be with me. I took a shuttering breath and wished like hell that the pain in my chest would ease.

Frankie fucking confused me.

I knew why she pushed me away. I had hurt her; she had been hurt so many times, and she was protecting herself.

I had given her reason to think that she needed to protect herself from me.

Everything about that was my fault, but the way she looked at me and the way she touched me made me believe that even though she was scared, she wanted this too.

Frankie wasn't the same girl that I had left behind. She was still everything that I loved about her, but she was also so different. She had grown and changed, and maybe this new version of her didn't need me.

The thought blasted into me as if someone had hit me, and even as I tried to breathe, I knew that truth would continue to hurt for a long time.

I couldn't imagine not needing her. I couldn't fathom a life where she and I didn't exist together.

And even though we had barely spoken the past year, I had always held on to hope. In the back of my mind, I always knew that it was her even when she told me that this couldn't happen.

Now I didn't know what to think.

I didn't know how the fuck I was supposed to change the way I felt.

I was already hurting Jordan, and the fact that she wasn't at the very front of my mind told me all I needed to know.

Even though I had told her everything about Frankie, she still wanted me. She wanted me, and I would continue to hurt her because I didn't know how to not love Frankie more than her.

And I wasn't sure if I loved her at all. I cared for her, sure, but it was so different. What I felt for her was so far from what I felt for Frankie that I couldn't compare the two. It wasn't fair.

My love for Frankie was all-consuming and irrational, but everything with Jordan was a choice. A choice to try to make myself get over Frankie, to move past her.

I looked out over the vastness of the ocean before turning back to the shore. I steadied my breath and readied myself to catch a wave. My fingers pressed into the sides of the board, and I leaned forward to drop back to my stomach, and that was when I saw her.

Frankie was standing on the beach directly in front of me with her arms wrapped around her chest. She was still wearing the exact same outfit as before, and her head was cocked to the side just slightly as if she was studying me.

We were so far apart from each other, but it didn't matter. I could still feel her, the sadness radiating off her. It beckoned me to her despite the words she had said before.

I dropped to my stomach and let my chest hit the board. A wave was forming behind me, so I paddled hard and fast to keep up with its speed, and I let my body take over as the wave began pushing me forward and I jumped to my feet. I caught the wave just in time and rode it as I stared ahead at Frankie.

She was still watching me, and she hadn't moved an inch, even though I feared she would disappear before I could get to her. I was so damn scared that she was going to vanish, and I was never going to be able to touch her, talk to her, love her again.

She had that power, and I knew I wouldn't blame her if that was what she decided.

If she chose Ben or whoever else she wanted to love. That was her choice to make even if it killed me. Because making choices for Frankie had never worked out for me before, and I knew that she hated it when we tried.

We had made her feel like a victim when she had been fighting not to become one.

She had been pushing me away again and again because I wasn't someone who made Frankie stronger. I made her weak. I made her question her choices and feel fragile in her want for me.

I was such a fucking idiot.

My board turned to the left, and I hit the rough water at the wrong angle, causing the nose of my board to bury into the water. I was flung forward and hit the water in a hard crash. In a weird way, that felt just as much like home as sitting on the board did.

I fell beneath the water and deep blue surrounded me for a few seconds. I didn't fight against it. I let it pull me under until the undercurrent was finished with me, and only then did I push back up to the surface.

I gulped down a deep breath before pushing the water and my hair out of my face. I opened my eyes and Frankie was still there. She was chewing on her thumb now, and I knew that was something she always did when she was nervous.

I hated that she felt that way around me. I hate that I had given her any reason to have any doubts because I didn't show her that she would always be my top priority.

The board was a few feet in front of me, and I swam forward and caught onto it before tucking it under my arms. I rested my chin against the board and stared up at Frankie.

She took a few steps toward the water before stopping again. "We should talk."

"Yeah." I nodded my head and pushed forward. "I'm listening."

"Can you get out of the water?"

"Can you get in?" I cocked my head to the side.

She shook her head before looking behind her, then she stared back at me. She hesitated for only a second longer before dropping her shorts down her legs. I couldn't see anything inappropriate because her shirt fell to the tops of her thighs, but she still tugged on the ends of it as if I hadn't seen every inch of her body last night.

"You really are a pain in my ass." She eased into the water, and the ocean lapped at her ankles like it was eager to greet her.

"That's okay." I nodded my head. "I feel the same way about you."

"Do you?" She cocked her head and moved deeper. Her thighs were touching the water now, and I could barely look away from her tan skin. It was such a unique color. So different from even her brother's, mom's, or dad's. It was as if the sun kissed her in a way that it had never done with anyone else.

And fuck, it was gorgeous.

"It depends on the day, honestly." I let my gaze roam over her as her legs disappeared in the water. "Sometimes I don't know what the fuck I'm feeling."

Frankie looked away from me as she crept farther into the water. "I feel that way about you most of the time."

"Unsure?"

"Warring." Her dark brown eyes came back to meet mine. "I feel like my heart and my head are always at war when it comes to you."

I knew exactly how she felt. I didn't have any uncertainties when it came to her, but I was confused about where the two of us worked together. If we ever would.

"And have they come to a conclusion?"

"No." She shook her head as she stopped on the other side of the board and put her hands on it just in between mine. "I'm more confused than ever."

"I'm sorry." I meant it sincerely. "I didn't mean to come here and fuck up things you have going for you. I didn't mean to fuck things up with Ben."

Frankie laughed softly and stared up at me. "Yes. You did."

"Okay. Maybe the Ben thing really fucking bothered me, but that wasn't my plan. It just hit me harder than I thought it would seeing you with someone else."

"Yeah." She ran her fingers over the board and moved the droplets of water around. "Now you know how I feel."

Because she had to see me with Jordan.

"When you came to California, I really wasn't with Jordan."

"That was over a year ago, Olly. It doesn't matter."

"Yes. It does." I ran one of my fingers over her knuckles. They were so fucking smooth. "I want you to know that I didn't lie to you. I would never lie to you. I didn't start seeing Jordan until months after you left, after you told me you didn't want this."

She nodded her head but was still staring down at the board. "That actually does make me feel a little better."

"What about Ben? Is that new?"

She looked back up at me then. "It is. I honestly barely know him."

"But you like him?" My chest ached and my heart raced as I waited for her answer.

"I think I do. And you like Jordan?"

I wasn't sure if it was a question or a statement, but I knew I needed to give her an answer either way. "Yeah."

She closed her eyes, and I hated the way I could feel her pain. Even as she tried to hide it from me, I knew that I was hurting her. "But not like you. What I have with her is nothing like you."

She bit down on her lip and looked back up at me. "That's not fair for you to say to me."

"But it's the truth."

"And what does she think is happening? Does she know that you're here right now with me?"

"Yes. She knows that I'm here." My heart was pounding out of my chest. "I told her that I still have feelings for you and that I was coming to see you."

"And does she know what we did last night?"

"Of course not. I wouldn't…" I almost said hurt her like that, but I did. Regardless of whether she knew or not, I was hurting her. "I already hurt her when I told her that I couldn't do things with her because of you. I'm not going to call and tell her what we did last night."

"I feel like we're still a secret, Olly." Frankie flicked her fingers through the water. "We've gotten older, we've grown apart, and still, we're this dirty little secret for each other."

"That's not true. I told Beck that I want to be with you."

She lifted her shoulders and let them fall. "Maybe that's all we are ever meant to be. You know? Maybe this" —she motioned back and forth between us— "would lose all of its allure if we ever became anything more."

"You honestly can't believe that." Please don't fucking believe that.

"I don't know. See." She tapped her head. "Still at war."

"Well, I don't believe it." I attempted to push the board out from between us, but her fingers clung to it and held it in place.

"I don't think you know what you believe, Olly. I think that you knew you were going to see me this weekend, and it fucked with your head. I think that you believe you owe me something that you don't."

"I think about you every day."

"Yet, you've moved on. I'm not mad at you for doing so. It's what you're supposed to do. It's what I told you to do. We live two completely different lives now, Olly."

"So, what? You just expect me to go back to California and pretend like this weekend never even happened? I'm supposed to pretend like I'm not going fucking crazy thinking about you?"

"I expect you to go home and finish your degree. Play the game. I know that you've been playing incredible. I watch every single game that I can. I will be nothing but a distraction from that."

"You won't."

"I will." Her eyes were pleading with me, and I didn't know what she wanted. But I felt like she was begging me to let her go even though I was dying for her to stay. "If you were with me, you would want to come here all the time and I would want to go there. That's something neither one of us has time for."

"So just continue living without each other?" I didn't

want to think about it. The last year had felt like torture. I didn't know how I was going to keep doing this without her.

"Just continue living." She smiled softly up at me. "Fall in love, Olly. Fall out of love. Go pro. Prove your parents wrong. Stop worrying about me."

She was pushing me away, and I didn't know if it was for her sake or mine. Either way, it was breaking me, and I wondered if this was how she had felt. Is this what I had done to her?

I reached out before she could stop me and cupped her cheek in my hand. She leaned into it before she could think better of it, and regardless of what she said, this girl would always be mine. She would always be the one who stirred something inside me that I was incapable of settling.

I couldn't stay away from her, and deep down, I knew that meant we weren't meant to be apart.

But if that was what she wanted, I would let her have it. I would give her anything I was capable of, even if it felt like it was killing me.

"Can I?" I leaned forward and pressed my forehead against hers. "Can I at least kiss you before you push me away completely?"

Her breath rushed out against my lips. "That's not what I'm trying to do."

"Yes. It is." My wet fingers ran down her cheek and along the line of her jaw. "You're trying to protect yourself from me because you no longer trust me." She shook her head softly, but I could see the truth in her eyes. "It's okay."

When she didn't answer, I pushed forward and closed the gap between us. My tongue slid along her mouth, and there was a hint of saltwater there. I didn't know if it was from her mouth or mine, but I licked it away before fully tasting her.

She moaned, the smallest sound that was almost washed away with the waves, but I felt like she was screaming at me. I cupped her cheeks with both of my hands and angled her face until she was looking directly up at me.

I ran kisses along her mouth before pressing in harder, and I sucked her tongue into my mouth when she pressed it against mine. I was so desperate for more. I was dying to feel her after everything she had just said.

I wanted to chase her words away from my memory and only think about them again when I was forced to remember that she was no longer mine. The board was still between us, and I wanted it gone. I wanted to destroy anything that kept me from her. But she was still clinging to it for dear life. She was holding on to it as if it could shield her from me.

But it couldn't.

I dropped my hands from her face and slid them beneath her arms. She blinked up at me for only a second before I lifted and pulled her torso onto the board.

"What are you doing?" She grabbed on to my arms to keep herself from falling forward, and I didn't stop. I kept pulling her toward me until she had no choice but to sit on the board with her legs dangling in the water in front of me.

"You're too far away."

"You said a kiss," she murmured and ran her fingers through my hair.

"And I'm not done kissing you."

I didn't give her time to think about it. I wrapped my hand around the back of her head and pulled her forward as I nestled between her knees, then I kissed her the way she should have been kissed her entire life. I kissed her with every bit of love and anger and hurt I felt, and I didn't hold one bit of it back.

She didn't either.

She met me every step of the way. We were a mess of lips and tongue and teeth, and her hands clung to me as hard as I held on to her. Neither of us was ready to let go.

We weren't ready for this to end.

I didn't think I ever would be.

My hands moved down her body, and I wrapped them around her hips. My fingers tangled into her wet t-shirt that was heavy with the saltwater and they ached to rip the damn thing off her.

"Olly," she whispered my name against my mouth, and I pulled away the smallest bit to look at her.

"Tell me what you want, Frankie. I won't take this any further than you tell me to."

I was telling her the truth. I would stop right now if that was what she wanted.

"I just..." She looked away from me, and I brought my hand back to her face and turned her gaze back to meet mine.

"Don't be ashamed to tell me what you want. Even if it's only for today. I'll give you whatever it is."

"Everyone went to the boardwalk." She whispered before glancing back up at me. "I just want to feel you one more time."

I didn't make her say any more. I kissed her again as I wrapped an arm around her back and brought her impossibly closer to me. She spread her legs, allowing me more room to fit between her thighs, and I tugged her closer to the edge of the board.

She was unsteady, the waves moving her around in front

of me, but I didn't care. I would chase her down regardless of where she went, and not even the fucking ocean could stop me.

Nothing could. Nothing except her.

"I need to taste you."

"Out here?" She chuckled, but I was already turning her and lifting one of her legs around the board. She straddled it before planting her hands against the tip of the board and staring up at me. "We cannot do this."

"If this is going to be goodbye, then I don't give a fuck where we are or who's watching." I gripped her calves in my hands and jerked her forward so quickly that she almost fell off the end. "Lay back, Frankie. I want to fuck you with my mouth."

"Oh God." Her legs shook, but she lowered to her back. I watched as her chest rose and fell rapidly, and her breasts heaved against her shirt.

I pushed her shirt up her stomach to reveal a thin pair of simple white panties, and I could see the outline of her pussy. I ran my tongue over my lips as I stared down at her. She was so perfect beneath me, so willing to give me exactly what I wanted in that moment, and I hated that this was temporary.

I would have given every bit of this up to have more. To have something other than sex with her.

Sex was nothing.

It was fucking amazing, but it was nothing.

Not in comparison to everything that she was.

"I'll give you whatever you want, Frankie." I was honest with her. "And I don't mean like this. I don't give a shit about the sex. If this is what you want from me, it's yours, but if you want more, if you ever want more, I'm yours."

But it was all that she was offering me, and right now, I was going to take what she would give.

I ran my fingers up her thighs, and she trembled beneath my touch as she stared up at me. I trembled too. I couldn't help it.

This felt like more. More than I should be taking, more than she should be giving, more than we were allowed.

But she didn't stop me, and she didn't reply. She just looked up at me with her dark brown eyes that were filled with things she said she didn't want.

It fucked with my head, but I didn't dare look away.

When my fingers met her pussy over her panties, I felt frantic with need. I gripped one side of her panties in my hand and tugged hard, and not a damn thing happened.

Frankie snorted hard with laughter, and she quickly covered her mouth as more laughter rang out.

I couldn't help joining her. "Are you laughing at me?"

"No." She nodded her head despite her answer. "It was just so freaking hot, and then..." She laughed again, and the board shook beneath her. "But then nothing happened."

"This is bullshit." I laughed alongside her, and my chest ached. This was what I missed. This right here was the exact moment I craved. "Lift your hips."

She did as I said even through her laughter, and I tugged her panties down her hips. She brought her legs back up onto the board, and I slowly slid the wet fabric down before tucking them into the pocket of my shorts.

"I can't believe that just happened." She was still laughing, and I smiled as I jerked her legs apart and pressed a kiss to the top of her pussy.

The laughter died on her lips, and her legs fell even harder at her sides. She opened for me, and I didn't hesitate as I ran my tongue through her pussy and tasted her. She bowed up off the board as my tongue hit her sensitive clit, and she reached behind her to grip the board above her head.

It gave me the perfect fucking view of her body, and I stared up at her breasts as her chest heaved with every swipe of my tongue.

"I've missed you so fucking much." I pressed my lips against her clit as I slowly slid two fingers inside her, and when she whimpered, I gently sucked. It was something she loved, she always had, and I loved the way her body reacted. Her legs clamped down around my head, and her eyes shot to mine. Her mouth was open but silent, and I wished she would just voice every damn thought that was running through her head. "You are so damn gorgeous."

I curled my fingers inside her over and over before slowly pulling out and thrusting them back in. She was so damn tight around them, and every time my tongue caressed her clit, she clenched down harder around me.

Her thighs were still pressed against me, and I lifted them one at a time in my hands before dropping them over my shoulders. I stared down at her pussy, so wet and ready for me, as my fingers slid in and out of her. I couldn't imagine not doing this again, not giving her pleasure like it was my biggest fucking honor.

Because it was.

The fact that Frankie trusted me at all to give her this, to touch her in this way, was more than I should have ever been given. She was more than I was worthy of.

She was more than anyone was.

Frankie was on a level all on her own, and as she looked

up at me with a mix of pleasure and lust staring up at me, I could barely handle it.

I brought my head back down to her and sucked her back into my mouth. This time, there were no gentle touches or teasing kisses. I fucked her with my mouth while my fingers fucked the inside of her, and every second that passed made me feel more starved.

I was willing to pour every bit of myself into her, but I wasn't sure how much of me would be left.

"Oh God, Olly." Her legs tightened around my shoulders. "I'm going to come."

I pumped in and out of her harder and faster, and I sucked her into my mouth. "Let go, Frankie. Come against my mouth."

She let go then, her body trembling around me, and I drank in every second of it. I let her ride it out against my mouth, and I didn't stop her until I knew she couldn't take any more. Only then did I raise my head and wrap my arm around her back to lift her to me. She almost fell off the board as she clung to my shoulders, but I didn't care.

I needed to kiss her. I was dying to have my mouth against her and feel more.

I wasn't ready to let her go.

I pushed my fingers through her wet hair and tugged at her scalp to hold her impossibly closer to me. She whimpered in my mouth and kissed me back as hard as I was kissing her. Her fingers dug into my sides, and she pulled me in.

I was so desperate not to let go of the other while we were saying goodbye. I knew that Frankie would always be a part of my life, but not this Frankie. Not this version of her that I had been so damn blessed to know.

I didn't know if I would ever have the pleasure of knowing her again, and I couldn't breathe when that thought crossed through my mind.

So, I kissed her harder.

I kissed and kissed her and tried to make sure she knew exactly how I felt. She was pushing me away, but I was going to love her regardless. Whether Frankie was mine or not, I would love her either way.

And that was the hardest part of all.

Because I knew that I wouldn't be able to get over this girl. She wasn't the kind of girl you ever got past. She was the one that haunted you in your dreams, the one you compared everyone else to, the one who felt like she was a lifetime ago but still within arm's reach all at once.

And I didn't want to give her up.

I pulled away from her and ran my fingers back through her hair as I stared down at her. She was looking up at me like she felt the exact same way about me, but I couldn't force her to want that. Regardless of how she felt about me, she had to want that for it to ever be real.

And I wasn't what she wanted.

Not now. Not anymore.

"I love you, Frankie." I leaned forward and pressed a soft kiss against her lips before dropping my hands and taking a step back from her.

"Wait." She reached out her hand, and I held no power to deny her. "Where are you going?"

I shook my head because I didn't know what to say. I didn't know how to give her what she wanted while also denying the way she was looking at me. "I'm going to go. I should stop by my parents' house."

"Olly, I…" She hesitated, and I held my breath.

Say you don't want me to go. Say you want me to stay, and I won't ever leave again.

That thought rolled over and over through my mind, and I knew how dangerous it was. This was exactly what she meant. We were both more than willing to give up everything for each other, and we shouldn't.

I had school and ball, and she had a fucking life.

A fucking life that didn't include me.

CHAPTER 10

FRANKIE

One Year Later

"Frankie, wake up. We're going to be late."

I blinked open my eyes and groaned as the bright light flooded the room. Why were we waking up so damn early? "What time is it?" I threw my arm over my eyes and tried to pull the blanket back over my chest.

"It's seven-thirty." Ben pulled the blanket back down my body and patted my hip. "Now get a move on or we're going to be late."

"Ugh." I practically growled at him before sitting up in his bed. He was already dressed in a pair of light gray slacks and a crisp white button-down shirt, and he looked so handsome. Far too handsome for seven o'clock in the morning. "Why are we up so early?"

He looked over at me with a soft smile, and I knew I probably looked like a damn mess. I was not seven a.m. pretty. It would never be my thing. "We're meeting our parents for breakfast this morning, remember?"

Shit. Our parents. As in his parents and mine, and they were meeting for the first time.

"Oh fuck." I jumped out of the bed and ran past Ben to get to the bathroom. He stopped me with his arm around my middle and spun me back until I was facing him.

"Not so fast." He chuckled and moved some of my errant hair out of my face. "Kiss me first."

"I haven't brushed my teeth."

"Don't care." He leaned down and pressed his lips against the corner of my mouth. "You're kissing me before you leave this room."

I smiled because Ben was always like this. We had just been dating for right at a year now, but he always had to touch me, to kiss me before I left him. It was endearing.

"Fine," I grumbled playfully and rolled my eyes just before his lips met mine. He kissed me gently, his tongue rolling softly against mine, and I pressed up on my tiptoes for more. I wanted him to kiss me harder, to bruise my mouth, to bruise anything. But the kiss was over as quickly as it started.

"Now go get ready." He slapped my panty-covered ass, and I smiled up at him before heading into the bathroom.

I closed the door behind me and took a deep breath. I was excited for our parents to meet, but I was also nervous. I was more nervous about my parents meeting his than I was about me meeting his parents.

I needed their approval more than I had realized. I needed them to tell me that I wasn't making a huge fucking mistake.

Ben and I weren't getting married or anything like that, but Ben had graduated. He had graduated, and he was staying here for me. That felt like more than any sort of engagement.

It felt overwhelming, and I just needed them to tell me that it was okay.

Because when I took a deep breath and closed my eyes, the only thought that flashed through my mind was Olly.

And thinking about him made me feel like I was making the biggest mistake of my life.

But when he wasn't there, when he wasn't flooding my brain, I really liked Ben. I may have even loved him.

But it was so different, and I hated that I was comparing him to Olly. He didn't deserve that. He didn't deserve what I did with Olly the first time I had brought Ben to Clermont Bay, but that felt like a lifetime ago.

It felt like it had been forever since I had touched or talked or felt Olly, but time didn't seem to matter.

Not when I was supposed to be living my life and he was supposed to be living his. Ben was everything I could have wanted, that I should have wanted, and I needed to remember that.

He wasn't Olly, but he was good for me.

But it was moments like this where I couldn't seem to push Olly back. I couldn't make myself forget him even when I tried.

I moved in front of the mirror and took a deep breath before washing my face. I quickly pulled myself together, taking time to do my makeup, and curling my hair, and when I looked in the mirror, I saw the girl Ben's parents would love.

They had to love me.

I pushed out of the bathroom and grabbed a pair of underwear from the top drawer of Ben's dresser. It was my drawer, and it wasn't lost on me that he had given me that. He wanted me, and he was willing to make so many changes to his life and his plans to have me.

He gave it all so freely and easily, and I should have never wanted more than he was giving me.

I pulled on my undergarments before putting on the soft pink sundress over my head. I barely recognized myself as I stared into Ben's full-length mirror, but when Ben walked up behind me, we looked so good together.

Ben and this girl, they fit together so perfectly, and he reminded me of that fact when he bent and laid a soft kiss against my shoulder.

"You ready?"

"Yeah." I nodded before pulling away and quickly sliding my feet into a pair of wedges. "Are you nervous?"

"No." He chuckled as he watched me. "Are you?"

"A little." That was a colossal lie.

"You have nothing to worry about." He gripped my fingers in his and pulled me from the room. "My parents are going to love you. "

"Yeah." I nodded again and chewed on my bottom lip. "We have nothing to worry about."

"Exactly." He held my hand as we left the apartment, and as he opened the car door for me. He only let it go for a moment while he moved into the driver's seat, then he was searching it out again. It should have calmed me, reassured me, but I just stared down at where our hands connected and felt more conflicted than ever.

We pulled up outside of the restaurant, and Ben grinned before lifting my hand to his mouth and kissing it. I smiled back, and I hoped that he didn't see through it.

I didn't want him to question my feelings for him when I

didn't know the answer myself. It wasn't that I didn't care for Ben, I did, but things were getting more serious and the weight of my choices was suffocating me.

I climbed out of the car when he opened the door, and we walked into the restaurant hand in hand. I spotted my parents almost immediately sitting at a large round table in the middle of the restaurant, and when my gaze met my mom's, I took a deep, grounding breath.

She saw it too. Her eyes narrowed as she stood, and I dropped Ben's hand to fall into her arms.

"Hi," she said softly against the side of my head as I held her to me.

"Hi."

She pulled me away from her, and she looked me over in a way that only a mother could. She could see every single detail that I hid from everyone else. She laid me bare right there in front of her, and I could see the many emotions passing over her face as she did.

"You live far too close to us for us not to see you in this long."

"I know." I nodded just as my dad stood to wrap his arms around me. I could see the way my father had aged in the way he stood and in the deep lines of his face. He was still one of the most handsome men I had ever seen.

"Frank." He held out his arms to me, and I scrunched my nose up at his nickname for me.

"Dad."

He pulled me into his arms with a soft chuckle before letting me go and turning toward Ben. "How are you, Ben?"

"I'm good, sir." Ben smiled and held out his hand in my father's direction. They shook hands, and I could tell my father was sizing him up like he always did. "How are you?"

"I'm good."

They dropped hands and Ben turned to my mom. "Mrs. Clermont, it's good to see you again. You look beautiful today."

A soft blush painted my mother's cheeks, and she stepped forward to pull Ben into a hug. "Oh please. I told you to quit calling me that."

Ben smiled as he held my mother against him, and his eyes softened on me.

"Oh. There are my parents." Ben held up his hand. "Excuse me for just a moment." He headed toward the entrance of the restaurant, and I watched as his mother's eyes lit up at the sight of him. His parents had traveled much farther than mine had, and I knew that they missed him.

"Are you okay?" My mom gripped my hands in hers, and I quickly turned back to look at her.

"Of course."

She chewed on her lip, a trait I had picked up from her, and I knew that she didn't believe me. But she didn't say another word about it as Ben and his parents made their way to the table.

"You guys, this is Frankie. Frankie, this is my mother, Heidi, and my father, Benjamin."

"It's so nice to meet you." I rushed forward and went in for a hug just as Ben's mom held out her hand. I didn't see it until it was too late, and I crushed her hand between us as I wrapped my arms around her. The hug was one-sided, mostly because her arm was currently between us, but I had to bite back my curse before I stepped back with a smile and held my hand out to his father.

"I'm the hugger," his dad joked with a wink and quickly pulled me into him.

I let out a deep breath and chuckled as I hugged him back.

"It's nice to meet you too, Frankie." He let me go with a soft pat on my back, then we did introductions with our parents before we all found our seats.

Ben was sitting to my left and my mother on my right, and I tried my hardest not to bounce my leg under the table so neither of them noticed. But of course, Ben did.

He laid his hand against my thigh and squeezed his fingers against my skin. He wasn't telling me to stop, just that he was here. He was here, and that was all that mattered.

That should have been all that mattered.

"So, Frankie," Ben's father leaned forward, resting his arms on the table. "You grew up around here? It's absolutely beautiful."

"Yeah." I nodded. "My parents are just a couple of towns over farther up the coast." I nodded toward my father. "They own a country club there."

"Oh, wow." He turned his attention to my father. "I'd say that's a handful."

"It is." My father chuckled. "That's why my son's taking over."

Both of them laughed before my father lifted his glass of water to his lips.

"That was my plan with Ben here, but he seems to have found something that's going to keep him away from Texas." His father smiled in my direction, and I tensed. I knew this was a sore topic for them. I had heard Ben on the phone arguing with them more times than I could count.

They thought he was making the wrong decision by staying here, and he didn't seem to care. That was how sure he was about me.

Guilt flooded me as I looked at his father. I was keeping their son here, and I wasn't sure about anything.

"Young love." My father chuckled again and wrapped his arm around my mother's shoulder. "It will make you do crazy things."

"Yes. It will." His mother smiled, but she didn't meet my eyes. She had barely looked in my direction the entire lunch. "We just want him to make smart decisions while he's in love."

Why was everyone talking about love?

I could feel the panic crawling up my chest as I stared down at my napkin. Our server was walking toward us with our lunch, and I felt like I was going to be sick. Ben had told me that he loved me once, and I hadn't returned the sentiment. I had panicked then just like I was panicking now.

I didn't know if I loved him. I wasn't sure how I was supposed to tell.

"Do you think it's a bad decision for him to stay here?" my mother asked his, and my gaze flew to her.

"No." His mother shook her head, but I could see the doubt in her eyes. "I'm just not sure if he's really thought things through."

"Can we not do this?" Ben tightened his hand on my thigh as he spoke to his mother. "This is your first time meeting Frankie, and I would like for it to be pleasant."

"Okay. Who ordered the blueberry pancakes?" our server interrupted them, and Ben's father raised his hand.

"That would be me."

Our server set his food in front of him before moving on and placing everyone's plate down. It all looked delicious, but I wasn't sure I could even manage a bite.

I stared down at my food as the conversation picked back

up and this time it was on to much lighter topics. Ben's father asked mine about golf, and my dad invited him back to the country club. His mom was silent as she ate, and I avoided looking in her direction altogether.

It wasn't that I thought she didn't like me, but I was sure that she didn't like the decisions Ben was making because of me. She thought that I was responsible for taking her son away from her.

My mom knocked her knee against mine under the table, and I looked away from shifting my food around my plate to look up at her. "I need to use the ladies' room. Come with me?"

"Yeah." I set my napkin down on the table and started to rise, but Ben quickly moved from his seat and pulled my chair out for me. "Thank you."

"Of course." He smiled at me before pressing a kiss to my forehead.

I didn't look to see if his mother was watching us. I couldn't bring myself to care. Instead, I followed my mom to the bathroom, and I took a deep breath as soon as the door closed behind us.

"Okay, spill." She spun in my direction and crossed her hands over her chest.

"Spill what?" I pushed into one of the stalls and locked the door behind me as I sat down to pee. I watched as her feet stopped directly in front of my door.

"What's going on with you? What's going on in your head?"

"There's nothing going on, Mom," I grumbled as I jerked some toilet paper off the roll.

"Frankie, I am your mother. You have never been able to

lie to me a day in your life, and you're not going to be able to start now."

I chewed on my lip before wiping and flushing the toilet. I situated my dress before I opened the door, and I squeezed past my mom to get to the sink. "I'm not lying to you. I don't know what you want me to say."

"Are you happy?" She cocked her head to the side and studied me as she leaned against the counter.

"What? Yes. I'm happy."

She narrowed her eyes, and I knew that she didn't believe me. But it was the truth. I was happy with Ben.

"As happy as you should be?"

I turned off the water and grabbed a paper towel. "What does that mean?"

"You know what I mean." She motioned toward me. "You are meeting your boyfriend's parents for the first time, and they are meeting yours. You should be thrumming with excitement and nervousness and happiness, but you look like someone kicked your puppy."

"No. I do not." I looked in the mirror, and I looked exactly like I should. I looked just like the girl I was trying to become.

"Frankie." My mom turned until she was fully facing me. "Talk to me."

I took a deep breath and looked at her. I didn't know what she wanted me to say, what I was supposed to say. If I said things that were running through my head out loud, I knew that would suddenly make them feel more real.

And then I wouldn't be able to bury my head in the sand anymore. I would have to fucking face the decisions I was making and the things I was desperately trying to push into the past.

"I just don't know if this is the right decision."

"If what is?" She leaned closer to me. "You're not getting married to Ben. Right?" She narrowed her eyes. "He hasn't proposed to you. Has he?"

"No." I shook my head and tried to push down the anxiety from her question. "But he's staying here because of me. He's staying here and that feels huge."

"It is huge." She shrugged her shoulders. "But that's his decision to make. You're not forcing him to stay against his will, Frankie."

"I know that." Of course, I knew that, but...

"Do you love him?" She asked the question I wished she hadn't. The question I had been trying desperately to avoid in my own head.

"I..." I bit down on my lip as I searched her eyes. "I honestly don't know."

"Okay." Her answer was short and hesitant.

"How do you even know if you love someone? Like is there a guide someone older and wiser is supposed to pass down?"

"No." She shook her head as she laughed. "There is no guide. You just know."

"That is literally zero help." I wadded the paper towel between my fingers before throwing it down in the trash can.

"You've been in love before." Her voice was much softer when she said that, and I knew that she was referring to Olly. Even as much as I had tried to hide how I felt about him from her, she had always known. "How did that feel?"

I shook my head as I thought about what she just asked. "Nothing like this."

I couldn't even compare the two. They were nothing alike. Not the way I fell or the way either of them picked me back up. Comparing Ben and Olly was impossible, and it was unfair.

Olly had been irrational decisions and secrets and intensity. Nothing about us had ever been what I was supposed to want. Olly was the guy that made me forget that I was ever supposed to care about anything outside of us.

But Ben was different. Ben chose me, and I was choosing him. He saw who I was, and he loved me so effortlessly. It didn't hurt with Ben. My chest didn't ache, and my heart didn't feel like it was constantly on the verge of being broken.

Olly was dangerous, and Ben was safe.

"Do you think it will ever feel like that?"

My mom winced, and I knew the answer without her saying a word.

"I don't know, baby. I just..." She pushed a lock of hair over my shoulder. "When was the last time you talked to Olly?"

My chest ached as his name passed her lips.

"Umm. It's been a while. Close to a year."

Her eyes almost bugged out of her head. "You haven't talked to him in a year? He's always been one of your best friends, Frankie."

"Things are a little different between us now, Mom. It doesn't matter anyway. This isn't about Olly."

"Isn't it?" Her hand ran over my jaw. "I think this is more about Olly than you care to admit."

She was right, of course, but I hated that she was. I didn't want how I felt about Ben to have anything to do with Olly. I just wanted... I wanted to forget about him for just a damn second.

But I couldn't. I never would.

And I didn't know if I could love Ben while I was still so in love with him.

"So, what am I supposed to do?" I held out my arms, and I prayed she gave me an answer. I needed her to tell me what to do.

"I don't know." She looked me over. "But you're supposed to be insanely happy, Frankie. If you're not that with Ben, then maybe he's not the guy for you."

My stomach sank at her words. I knew she was right, but I didn't want her to be. Being with Ben was easy. The two of us worked so well together. There was none of the constant chaos that was me and Olly.

I should have wanted easy. I did want it.

"I can be insanely happy." I squared my shoulders as I looked at my mom, and I saw the sadness in her eyes. It didn't matter how much I was convincing myself. She didn't believe me.

"Why don't you try to talk to Olly?"

"Olly scares me," I said the thing out loud that had been eating at me for so long. "I know that no matter what happens with Ben, I will be okay at the end of it, but I wouldn't be with Olly."

"Frankie." My mom reached out for my hand, and I let her take it.

"I don't like how easily I lose myself in him. Olly has the power to destroy me if he wanted to, and I don't want to give him that power."

"Oh, baby." She pushed my hair out of my face as I tried to swallow down the emotion that was threatening to drown me. "That's what love is."

"But I pushed Olly away because I was scared." Regret flooded me, and it was a feeling I had become so used to. "I pushed him away, and he's still dating Jordan. It's not fair to him."

"So, what do you want to do, Frankie?"

"I don't know." I shook my head because I didn't have a fucking clue. Every decision I made felt like the wrong one.

"Okay." She nodded and opened the door. "Then let's get back out there and get to know Ben's parents. You don't have to figure everything out in this bathroom, but you owe it to Ben to go back out there."

I took a deep breath and looked back in the mirror one last time. She was right.

"All right." I nodded as I still stared at myself and told one more lie. "I'm ready."

CHAPTER 11
OLLY

I stepped out of the locker room and smiled when I spotted Jordan leaning against the wall. She was wearing one of my jerseys, and she had the biggest smile on her face as she looked up at me.

"There he is." She grinned, and I made my way over to her.

"Have you been waiting out here the entire time?" I dropped my bag down beside her feet.

"Of course." She wrapped her arms around my neck. "I had to beat off all the groupies that were waiting out here to get a piece of the MVP."

She was full of shit. There wasn't a single other person in the vast hallway, and I knew there hadn't been. She was just here for me.

And I adored that about her.

"I'm sure there were so many." I wrapped my arms around her back, and she smiled even bigger.

"A swarm of girls. They were all chanting your name. It was good practice for when you go pro."

"*If* I go," I corrected her.

"You will." She leaned up on her tiptoes and pressed her lips against mine. "I know you will."

"I think you have too much faith in me." I pulled away from her and scooped up my bag before grabbing her hand in mine. "But I appreciate it."

She blushed before tucking a piece of her hair behind her ear. "Allie said that we're supposed to meet them at the restaurant. They were going ahead to get a table."

"Okay. Let's go." I wrapped her hand in mine and pulled her behind me. I felt genuine excitement about today, and it had been a while. Not only had we just won our playoff game that we were predicted to lose, but Beck and Josie were in town.

It felt like it had been forever since I'd seen them.

Jordan kept her hand in mine the entire ride to the restaurant, and she only let go long enough for us to climb out of the car. Her hand fit in mine so perfectly, and I smiled down at her as she shifted at my side.

"You okay?"

"Yeah." She nodded, but I could see her anxiety through her shield. "I'm just nervous."

I stopped before we got to the door and turned to face her fully. "Nervous about what?"

"Your friends." She motioned into the restaurant where I knew they were waiting on us. "I know that Carson doesn't really care for me, and I'm worried that Beck will be the same. I know he's important to you."

"Carson likes you." It was a half-lie. He had his moments. He just didn't love her for me. "And Beck will too."

"I know that he's Frankie's brother." She turned her gaze away from me as she said her name, and it took my breath from my chest. Why did she have to talk about her? Why did she have to mutter the one name I had been desperate not to think about? "I feel like they are going to compare everything I do to her."

I was the one who planted this doubt in Jordan. When I had come home from Clermont Bay after my last visit over a year ago, I had told her everything. Well, almost everything. Most importantly, I told her I was still in love with Frankie and that I wasn't sure there would ever be a time that I wasn't.

But Jordan stayed.

She was willing to fight for us when all I could think about was someone else. She wanted to love me when I wasn't sure I would ever love her.

And that was so fucked up.

But I did love Jordan. I loved her in a way that mattered more than I thought it ever would, but it still... I... she wasn't Frankie.

And I didn't know if I would ever be able to love anyone the way I loved that girl. Even after not talking to her for the last year. I was still so madly in love with her that it hurt to think about.

She was still with that guy, and I was still here with Jordan.

We were in two different worlds, but it didn't matter. The way I felt for her was as strong as ever, and all I could do was push it down. She chose Ben.

She chose a life that didn't include me, and I had to accept that.

I had to fucking move on even though it felt so damn impossible.

Because Frankie wasn't waiting for me. She wasn't

worried about what I was doing or not doing, and it was fucking stupid that I felt immense guilt every time I touched Jordan. It was even worse that I still thought about her. Every time I touched Jordan, Frankie still flashed through my mind, and she was always the image I had in my head when I got off.

It was so fucked up, and Jordan didn't deserve that.

But I didn't know how to make it stop. If I could quit loving Frankie, even for a second, I would try. I would do whatever I could to move on from the girl who had clearly moved on from me.

"They are not going to compare you to Frankie." I pressed my fingers against her chin and turned her head until she was looking at me. "Frankie is my past."

"But..." She hesitated, and I knew she was going to say something about me still loving her. She wanted to love me regardless, but she hadn't forgotten what I said. I was sure that she never would.

"They are going to love you. Just be the girl that I love."

A small smile formed on her lips, and she blinked up at me. "Okay."

She took a few deep breaths before I spoke again. "Are you ready?"

"Yeah." She nodded, and I wrapped my hand back around hers and pulled her into my side as we pushed through the door of the restaurant.

I could hear Carson's loud laughter as soon as we entered, and I kept Jordan at my side as we moved through one of my favorite restaurants in search of my friends.

"Olly!" Carson cheered as we spotted them and he lifted a beer in our direction. "Our all-star has finally arrived."

I rolled my eyes and pulled out a chair for Jordan before taking the seat beside her.

"You make one good play and all of a sudden you're trying to give me a big head."

"One good play, my ass." Carson leaned forward and grinned. "You, my dear boy, played the game of your life tonight."

He set an ice-cold beer down in front of me, and I lifted it just in time to clink the bottle against his.

"Thanks, man." I took a long swig of the beer and tried to calm my nerves. He was right. I had played the game of my life, but I wasn't a fan of having all the attention on me. I wiped the back of my hand against my mouth and looked over at Beck.

"Beck, this is Jordan." I turned toward her and wrapped my arm around the back of her chair. "Jordan, that's Beck, and that's Josie. Josie, Jordan."

I could see Josie already staring at Jordan, measuring her up to what she thought I deserved, but her eyes softened as I introduced them, and she smiled. "It's nice to meet you, Jordan. I feel like I've been hearing about you forever."

"You too." Jordan laughed. "I was starting to believe you all weren't real."

"You didn't think Olly and I had any other friends."

"I'm your friend, asshole," Garrett said just as he walked up and took the seat to my left.

"I meant from back home." Carson rolled his eyes.

"Honestly, if Allie hadn't talked about them, then yeah, I was starting to think you all made them up."

I snorted out a laugh and took another sip of my beer.

"We're real." Beck laughed too. "This group has been through a lot of shit together."

"Facts." Carson pointed at him with laughter. "Probably too much, honestly."

"You three were too much." Josie looked at each of us. "Us girls were perfect angels."

"Bullshit." Beck looked over at his girl. "You all were the bad influences."

"Oh, please." Allie rolled her eyes before shoving a chip into her mouth.

"I wish Frankie was here. She'd put your ass in your place." Josie laughed, and I felt like everyone at the table suddenly became quieter as my chest ached.

Jordan went completely stiff beside me, and I hated that. Frankie wasn't even here, and she was still so affected simply by her name.

Carson looked at me quickly before turning back to Josie. "How is Frankie anyway? I feel like I haven't talked to her in forever."

"That's because you don't ever call anyone but Allie." Josie made a face at him before continuing. "She's good. Just focused on school."

"And her boyfriend," Beck said so flippantly that I was certain he had no fucking clue how much his words were affecting me. "I think they're actually getting kind of serious. She stays at his place all the time, and Mom and Dad went to meet his parents last weekend."

"What?" Carson asked the question that I almost blurted out myself.

"Yeah." Beck nodded. "I wasn't sure about him at first, but he seems like a good enough guy."

A good enough guy? A good enough fucking guy?

My temper rose as he spoke, and I was so close to saying something that I knew I would regret. He was perfectly fine with a good enough guy dating his sister, but his best friend hadn't been good enough.

He didn't give me a fucking chance to be good enough for her.

And that fact infuriated me.

I stared down at my beer as I tried to get my anger under control. It felt useless. They were still talking around me, but all I could think about were the words that Beck had just said. Over and over, they flew through my mind.

"Is this the same guy that was at your birthday party when we came into town?" I knew it was. I had seen his face plastered all over her social media, and I had no idea why I asked the question. I just couldn't get past what he had just said.

"Yeah." Beck nodded as he looked at me. "Ben's his name."

I didn't give two shits what his name was. But of course, I knew it. Who the fuck could forget the name of a man who was allowed to love the woman I was still in love with?

"What's he do?" *Shut up, Olly.*

"He just graduated with his business degree. He was supposed to move back to Texas to help his dad, but I think he's planning on sticking around with Frankie."

Fuck. He was staying. He was staying with her when I left.

There was no question in my mind as to why she chose him over me. She chose him because he made it perfectly fucking clear that he chose her.

"And you like him?"

I felt Jordan tense at my question, and I finally looked over at her. She was looking anywhere but at me, and I was such an asshole. This wasn't a conversation I should be having in front of her. Hell, it wasn't a conversation I should have been having at all, but I was so angry.

"I don't know if I'd go that far." Beck ran his hand over the back of his neck as he looked at me, and I knew he could see my anger staring back at him. "But he's good to her, and she seems happy."

I made her happy too. It was on the tip of my tongue, but I bit it down so hard that I could taste the coppery flavor of my own blood.

"What about you guys?" Josie looked back and forth between me and Carson. "Do you think you're going to move home as soon as you graduate?"

"Yes." Carson's answer was instant and so sure. But I didn't know.

"It depends." I finally answered when she turned her attention back to me.

"On?" Her eyes glanced in Jordan's direction, and I winced because Jordan had never really been part of the equation.

"Baseball mostly." I was honest. "If I get drafted, then I'll have to go wherever that is. If not..." I shrugged my shoulders and took a deep breath as I tried not to think about that possibility. "I don't know what I'll do."

"What about you, Jordan?" Josie turned her attention to her. "Are you from here?"

"Yeah." Jordan cleared her throat as she nodded her head. "My family is just about thirty minutes south."

"Well, I'm not going back to Georgia," Garrett said with a laugh. "So one of you fuckers are going to have to give me a room in one of your mansions."

"I don't live in a mansion," Allie said as she leaned into Carson. "But I'd take you in, Garrett."

Garrett grinned and Carson rolled his eyes. "Don't get a big head. She takes in any strays she finds."

"Including him." Allie laughed and patted Carson on the chest. "My favorite stray of all."

"Funny." Carson leaned down and pulled Allie into a kiss.

Jordan shifted awkwardly beside me, and I leaned in closer to her.

"You okay?" I whispered close to her ear for only her to hear, and she quickly nodded.

She still wasn't looking at me, and I knew that I fucked up. I should have never let Beck's words get to me. I should have never allowed her to see how worked up I still got over someone else.

But I had, and I didn't know how to make it better. I couldn't take it back. Not the way I reacted or the things I had done with Frankie the last time I saw her. I couldn't take back the hundreds of things I had done that hurt Jordan.

I couldn't take back the fact that I knew I would walk away from Jordan so easily with only a word from Frankie.

I wished I wasn't able to admit that to myself so easily. I wished more than anything that it wasn't the truth, but it was.

I leaned forward and closed the gap between us, and I pressed my lips against Jordan's temple as I closed my eyes. She smelled so good, the light scent of flowers hitting me as I ran my nose along her skin.

Jordan was kind and funny, and she didn't deserve to be my second choice. She deserved far more than I was currently giving her, but I didn't know how to give her something that no longer belonged to me.

Jordan finally looked up at me and gave me a soft smile

that didn't quite reach her eyes. I hated that I was hurting her and that no matter how hard I tried, I couldn't seem to stop.

I brought my mouth down to meet hers, and I kissed her. I tried to erase everything I had just said and everything I had made her feel with one simple kiss, but I knew that it was impossible.

My love for Frankie was becoming as real for her as it was for me, and neither one of us could escape it.

"Let's order shots!" Carson cheered, and I pulled away from Jordan just enough to look down at her.

She smiled at me again, this one stronger than the one moments before, and I tried to look at her the exact same way. I tried to show her with my eyes what felt impossible for me to say, and I hoped that she believed me.

"You want a shot?" I murmured against her mouth as I went in for another kiss.

"Yeah." She chuckled and nodded her head.

"That's my girl."

CHAPTER 12
FRANKIE

"Oh my God, no!" I laughed as I ran from Ben, but he was too fast. He caught up to me before I ever stood a chance, and threw me over his shoulder.

"I thought you were a water girl." He chuckled as he hiked me higher on his shoulder and started walking.

"The ocean, Ben! Water you can see through. I don't swim in a murky lake in Texas!"

He wasn't listening to me. His hands tightened around my thighs, and he continued to push forward toward the edge of the boat. Water where alligators and giant fish and who the hell knew what else lived.

"We're jumping off this boat, Frankie. So you better hold your breath."

I watched as his friend laughed, and I tried to reach out for him to hold on for dear life, but he was just out of reach.

"I don't want to be eaten! I'm too young!" I wrapped my arms around his torso and pressed my face against his back. I was going to kill him.

"Last warning!" he yelled just before he jumped off the

boat and a scream rang out around us. My scream of absolute terror.

We hit the water with a hard crash, and I clamped my eyes closed as I pushed off his body and did everything in my power to swim back to the surface as fast as I could. The water was warm and felt delightful, but that didn't make it any less scary.

I was one hundred percent sure that I was not a lake girl. Hell, I wasn't a Texas girl.

I broke through the surface and took a deep breath as I looked around me. The boat was to my left and Ben came up laughing to my right. I ignored him completely and swam as fast as I could to the damn boat.

We were in the middle of the lake in the middle of nowhere, and there was no way in hell I was just chilling there waiting for something to pull me under.

I grabbed a hold of the ladder and climbed out as Ben called out my name behind me. I didn't look back at him until I was safely back aboard the boat, and I narrowed my eyes at the shit-eating grin on his face.

"That was not funny." I pointed at him and his smirk intensified.

"I mean, maybe a little." He held up his thumb and forefinger, and I narrowed my eyes further. "Push her back in, Shawn. I didn't get to hold her or anything."

I turned my attention to Shawn, but he hadn't moved an inch. He was just laughing at his friend. "Shawn, I know we barely know each other, but I will kill you."

He held up his hands in surrender as he laughed. "Noted."

"You're no fun." Ben climbed up the ladder and shook his hair out of his face as water dripped off him.

I took a step back and took my seat at the front of the boat before Ben could grab me again. He followed me every step of the way and grinned. He leaned down as I sat, and water dripped from his body to mine as he got in my space.

"You aren't really mad at me, are you?" His mouth was so close to mine, and when I looked at the way he was smiling at me, it was hard to remember why I was angry in the first place.

"Yes. I am." I crossed my arms over my chest and his gaze immediately dropped there. There was a shift in his gaze that promised things that wouldn't be happening in front of his childhood friend, and I shifted in my seat. "If I had been eaten by an alligator, I would have never forgiven you."

He chuckled before leaning forward and pressing his lips to mine. I let him, of course, I did, and I loosened up the smallest bit.

"I would have never let anything happen to you. You know that, right?" He smiled and looked so sincere, and it was on the tip of my tongue to be honest with him. But I had only ever trusted one man explicitly.

"You can't see in that water, and you cannot fight off an alligator."

He chuckled at my answer and pushed some hair out of my face. "You don't think I'm strong enough to take on an alligator."

"No," I blurted out as he laughed. "Especially not in the water."

"I mean, you're right." He shrugged his shoulder and dropped another soft kiss against my lips. "But I would at least try."

He dropped down in the seat beside me and ran a towel over his face then his perfectly fit body. "What time is it?"

"Three," Shawn said as he looked down at his watch.

He was nice enough even though he barely spoke to me, but Ben had assured me that he was just a quiet person. If he hadn't, I would say the guy didn't like me.

But that seemed to be a going trend around here.

"We should probably head back." Ben pushed his sunglasses back on his face and leaned back beside me. "I promised my mom we'd be back in time for dinner."

Awesome. Another dinner where I basically just talked to his father. It wasn't that his mom wasn't nice. She was, but in the two months since I first met her, she had barely warmed up to me.

But Ben still hadn't decided to move back to Texas, and I knew she wouldn't be happy until he did.

I didn't blame her.

Shawn started the boat back up, and Ben grabbed my hand in his as we started to move along the water and the wind whipped past us. This part of the lake I liked. The scenery, the freedom of feeling the deep heat of the air, and the kiss of the sun along my shoulders.

I could do this all day.

I leaned back and closed my eyes as the sun pressed down against my face, and I took a deep breath. I had been so tense since we first arrived to Texas, and I tried my hardest to let that stress slip from me.

This was something I was going to have to get used to if I was going to be with Ben. This was his home, his family, and I didn't have to love them but I needed to at least tolerate them. I hated that word. I didn't want to tolerate anything. I wanted to love his mom. I was desperate for her to at least like me.

I wanted to be excited about being here. I should have

been ecstatic about seeing all the things that had made Ben, Ben. Instead, I just craved home. I felt homesick, and we had only just left.

But even when I was there, I still felt homesick somehow. There was a constant twinge in my gut that something wasn't right or something was missing, and I tried my hardest to push it away every time I felt it. If I thought too hard, if I really let it form, I would know exactly what it was that was pulling at my gut.

Exactly who it was.

And I couldn't think about him. Not without spiraling in a way that I knew wasn't good for me.

Because he wasn't good for me.

Olly had been one of the best things to happen to me in my entire life, but he also wasn't. Everything about us had always been on the edge of toxic. It was beautiful and life-changing, but it was also heartbreaking and hidden and deceptive.

Olly and I had never known how to be anything other than each other's crutch, and I didn't want that. I didn't want to fall to him when I felt like I could no longer hold myself up, and I didn't want to be that for him either.

I had wanted to be more. I had been desperate to be more.

And now she was. She was his more and Ben had become mine.

And I needed to accept that.

I was trying so fucking hard to accept that.

The boat slowed, and I blinked my eyes back open as the sharp sunlight flooded my senses. We were pulling back up at the dock just behind Ben's parents' house, and it looked so picture-perfect. There wasn't a single thing out of place as I stared up at their house. The backyard was covered in bright florals and a perfectly manicured lawn, and I almost felt guilty as we climbed out of the boat and stepped onto it.

Ben handed me my large bag, and I shoved my towel inside as I pulled out my phone.

I hadn't had service for hours while we were out of the lake, so I quickly clicked on the screen to see if I had missed anything.

There were a few missed texts and one news article that was sent to me by my brother. I almost ignored it completely until I saw Olly's name in the headline.

Local Clermont Bay resident, Olly Warner, drafted by Colorado Rockies

My breath rushed out of me and my hand trembled as I tried to hold my phone. I dropped my bag on the grass and scrolled through the article as fast as I could. It didn't say much that I didn't already know. They called Olly an outstanding player and a student at the top of his class.

There were a few quotes from him mostly just saying how excited he was to become a Rockie at the end of his season. Then there was a picture. He had the biggest grin on his face and a Rockies hat on his head, and he looked so damn handsome.

He did it. He fucking did it.

He was only a junior, but I wasn't surprised that it didn't take him his full four years to be drafted.

And now he was going to be moving to Colorado.

My gut sank, and I struggled to catch my breath. I didn't know why that fact hit me so damn hard. He was across the damn country from me now, and Colorado was technically closer. But it didn't feel like it.

It felt like he was moving farther and farther out of my

reach, and it hit me then that every bit of success Olly had only took him further away from me.

It didn't matter that this was what I had told him I wanted. Olly making it pro felt like it made things even more final for us.

"You okay?" Ben touched my elbow and I jumped.

"Oh, yeah." I pressed my hand to my chest.

"What's wrong?" He wrinkled his brow, and it ate at me that he was so concerned about me when I wasn't even thinking about him.

"Nothing's wrong." I shook my head and lifted the phone where he could see. "I just found out that Olly is going pro." Ben didn't know anything about Olly other than that he had been one of my best friends growing up. That was the understatement of the century, but I had never been able to bring myself to really tell him the truth.

I couldn't imagine that Ben would still want to be with me if he knew how much Olly still occupied my thoughts.

"Hell yeah." He grabbed my hand in his and quickly glanced over the article. "That's so cool."

"I know." I nodded. I always knew that he would make it, but I never really thought about the possibility of where his dream would take him. I never imagined that he would be so far from me. "I'm going to call and congratulate him." I tilted my head up to the house. "Why don't you go ahead? I'll be there in just a second."

"Okay." He smiled and reached down to grab my bag. "I'm going to go ahead and get changed." He pressed a kiss to my lips before he and Shawn walked away as they talked.

I held my phone in my hand and stared down at it as I started pacing in the grass. I wanted to call him. I owed him a fucking congratulatory call, if nothing else.

I was his friend. I had always been.

And I was so insanely proud of him.

My finger hovered over his name, and I watched as it trembled. I hadn't spoken to him in so long. It felt like it was forever ago yet yesterday at the exact same time.

I pressed his name before I could talk myself out of it and brought the phone to my ear. It rang and rang, and just as I was about to hang up, his voice came through the phone.

It was enough to take my breath away.

Just one simple word muttered from his lips. "Frankie."

I was silent for a long second as I tried to remember how to talk. "Hi."

His deep sigh echoed through the phone, and I imagined he had been holding his breath just like I had. Had he been missing me like I was missing him? Was he going crazy thinking about me?

"I just wanted to call you and tell you congratulations." I rushed out my words before I said something that I couldn't take back. "Of course, no one is surprised, but I'm still so insanely proud of you."

"Thank you." I could hear him shifting on the other end of the phone, and I tried to imagine what he was doing. Was he alone? Was he with her? Was he wishing I didn't call?

"I don't want to keep you or anything. I'm sure you have a ton going on."

"I haven't heard your voice in so fucking long."

I closed my eyes and begged my chest to stop aching. Please don't let every word the man utters gut me.

"I know." I shook my head even though he couldn't see it. "It feels like it's been forever."

"How are you?" His voice was so soft and so sincere, and I knew that he truly wanted to know. That was the thing about

Olly. He had always cared more about others than he ever did himself.

"I'm good." I planted a smile on my face and tried to make myself believe it. I looked back up at the house, but Ben had already disappeared from view. "But I'm not calling to talk about me. How does it feel? All your dreams are coming true, Olly. Is it everything you thought it'd be?"

He chuckled softly, and I imagined him running his fingers through his hair. "Honestly, it doesn't feel real. I have a few more games with my college team before the year is over, but then I'll be heading to Colorado. I've never even been to Colorado before."

"What are you going to do without any beaches?"

"I don't know." He laughed harder. "What am I going to do without you?"

Don't.

I slammed my eyes shut again and pressed my hand against my stomach. "You've been without me for quite some time, Olly."

"I know. Fuck, I know that. It just…"

"It feels more final," I finished the sentence for him.

"Yeah." There was another moment of hesitation. "It just feels like we're so far apart."

"It's okay." I shrugged and tried to sound like I believed what I was saying. "I'm sure we'll see each other soon, and you can tell me all about what it's like to be a big-shot baseball player. I'm sure Jordan is so excited for you and will be by your side."

I could feel tears welling in my eyes, and I didn't know what was wrong with me. He hadn't been mine in so damn long, and he had been hers for far longer. But that didn't seem to matter.

Not when my chest ached, and every single part of me still felt like it belonged to him.

"She is excited." There was such uncertainty in his voice. "But I'm not sure if she's coming with me or not."

"What?" I lifted my hand and chewed on the side of my thumb. "Why not?"

"I don't know, Frankie. She still has school, and…"

I wished I was there with him so I could touch him. I wanted to run my fingers over his face and smooth the deep line I knew was forming between his brows through his frustration.

"I'm honestly not sure about anything."

"I probably shouldn't have called."

"No." He said the word so quickly. "I'm glad you did. It's nice to hear your voice."

"I know, but I don't want you to feel like you owe me anything, Olly. I'm happy for you. I truly am."

"I don't feel like I owe you something. I just… I feel like I can't seem to move on."

He was being so honest, and it was gutting me. Every piece of truth that passed through his lips was like a weapon he could wield so easily.

And they hit their mark with perfect precision.

Because I knew exactly how he felt. I was trying to move on from him, but it felt like I was floundering most of the time. There were those very rare days, where a thought of him didn't cross my mind, but even on those, he was all I could see when I closed my eyes.

It was both heaven and hell.

"I know." It was the only thing I could think to say. I didn't know how to tell him that I hadn't moved on from him at all. He was with her, and I was with Ben, and it wasn't fair to either of them.

"How are you and Ben?"

I took a deep breath and looked out over the calm water of the lake. "We're okay. He's good to me, and honestly, what more could I ask for?"

"Hmm."

I thought about the words that had just left my mouth and scrambled to take them back. "I didn't mean it like that. Like you weren't."

"But I wasn't." He let out a deep laugh that held no humor. "God, Frankie. If I could go back and change things."

"But we can't." I needed the reminder myself.

"No. We can't, but..."

"But what, Olly?"

"I would choose you, you know. If that was what you wanted. I would choose you over her, over going pro, over all of it."

I clamped my eyes closed and tried to get a handle on myself. I knew that he would and that was the problem. Olly would give up everything for me now, but that wasn't what I wanted.

Going pro was his dream, and I didn't want to take that from him. He would regret it, and I never wanted him to regret me again.

"Olly," I whispered his name, and I wished I was anywhere but where I was. Ben was just a short walk away, and here I was falling apart over someone else. Someone I had no business falling apart over. But it was on the tip of my tongue to tell him that I would choose him too, I would choose him and go wherever he wanted me to go.

Because I knew that homesick feeling in my gut was for him.

I wanted him, and I had been an idiot for so long. I was going to tell him.

"Hey." His voice was muffled as if he was holding his hand over the phone. "Yeah. Give me just a second to get off the phone." There was a long pause as if he was listening to someone else, and I wondered if it was Jordan. "I love you too."

Oh my God. What was I doing? What in the actual fuck did I think I was going to accomplish with this conversation?

I had pushed him away, and he was in love with someone else. I pushed him away, and I didn't get to do this to him again.

"Frankie." He came back on the line, and I was already heading up to the house where Ben was waiting for me.

"I need to go, Olly."

"Frankie, wait."

"I'm so proud of you. You're going to be so amazing. I'll have to order myself some Rockies gear soon."

"Frankie, please." There was a desperation in his voice, and I felt that same desperation in my chest.

"Ben's waiting for me. I need to go." I didn't wait for him to say anything else. I knew I wouldn't be able to handle it. I wouldn't be able to face whatever he was going to say to me when I knew that he loved her.

He loved her, and I had already known that. Of course, I had, but it was different before. Before I heard him say those words to her.

I pressed End before I did something stupid, and I clenched my phone in my hand. The door opened behind me, and I turned around to find Ben watching me.

"Everything okay?" He shielded his eyes from the sun as he watched me, and I forced myself to take a step in his direction.

"Yeah." I nodded and tried to push Olly back down. I tried to force him from my every thought long enough for me to be the girl Ben knew.

"Then come on!" Ben smiled and waved me toward him. "My parents are waiting on us."

I planted a smile on my face and made my way up to him. He wrapped his arms around me as soon as I was in arm's reach, and guilt flooded me.

CHAPTER 13

OLLY

The pain was absolutely excruciating.

That's all I could think about as my coach squatted down in front of me and talked. I could barely hear a word he was saying. Not really. It all felt like a giant fucking blur as the intense throbbing seared through my knee.

I slammed my eyes shut as another shot of pain sliced through me.

I wasn't even sure how it happened. One second, I was covering the base, and the next thing I knew, the runner was sliding into me, and I felt an intense and sudden pop in my knee.

I couldn't stand. I sure as fuck couldn't walk. I could barely think.

"We're going to have to carry him off the field." One of the team trainers was talking to my coach, but their words were finally hitting me.

"Do you think it's torn?"

"Yeah." The trainer nodded his head with a wince, and my coach let out a string of curses.

Not only was he losing one of his star players in the middle of playoffs, but this was also going to screw up my commitment with the Rockies. I hadn't even signed the official contract yet.

Panic flooded me, and I looked around at all the faces that surrounded me until I met Carson's. He was looking at me with pity and anger, and I knew that he had come to the same realization that I had.

Everything I had ever wanted was completely fucked.

"Let's get him off the field." Coach moved to one side of me, but Carson pushed forward to the other side before anyone else could. The trainer tried to get to my side, but Carson refused.

"I've got him." He wrapped his arm around my torso and lifted me up at the same time Coach did. Pain sliced through my knee as I tried to hold the weight off my foot, and I groaned as I tried to hide it. "I've got you."

Carson took more of my weight into his side, and I leaned on him for support as they helped me off the field. The crowd in the stands clapped softly as we made our way off, and I hated it. I understood the sentiment, but what the fuck were they clapping about?

I had just lost everything in one small moment in time.

I looked up in the crowd just behind the dugout in time to catch a glimpse of Jordan. She had been crying and her hand was covering her mouth as she watched me struggle to get off the field.

The pity in her eyes was blaring, and so was the ring I put on her finger. A ring that had felt more like an ultimatum than a promise.

Carson had told me how stupid I was being, but I hadn't listened.

And I hadn't regretted it until Frankie called me just a few days after it happened. She called me about going pro, but when congratulations passed her lips, instant regret hit me when I thought she was talking about the engagement.

But she didn't have a clue, and I had been too big of a fucking coward to tell her.

I hadn't even expected to hear from her. It had been over a year, and she had made it clear the last time that I saw her that she wanted her space. And I gave it to her.

I gave her what she asked for, and everything inside of me regretted it.

I regretted it when Jordan told me that she couldn't stay with a guy who was still in love with someone else, and I hated that in my panic of losing her too, I made a decision that I never should have.

I was so fucking scared of being alone that I was clinging to Jordan like she was my lifeline. I craved the sense of security I felt with Frankie, and I was desperately trying to find it in her.

I was carelessly trying to fill the hole that Frankie had left, but it was impossible.

"Let's get him up on the table." Coach guided Carson as we moved into the locker room, and I gritted my teeth as my knee screamed in pain when they lifted me. "Are you okay?" Coach looked me in the eye, and I shook my head.

"No. I'm not fucking okay." I fisted my hands at my sides and tried to calm myself down.

It felt like everything was hitting me at once. All the mistakes I had made. All the bad decisions.

But flashes of them all faded and faded, and all that was left was her. Nothing else mattered. It didn't compare.

"Look at me." Carson grabbed my face and forced me to look up at him. "You're going to be fine. This can be fixed."

"I know." I nodded in unison with him. "But Colorado isn't going to sign a brand-new player with a blown-out knee," I stated the fact that everyone else was thinking.

If I had signed the contract a week ago, things would be different right now. I wouldn't be stressing out about the fact that Jordan didn't renew her lease and that she had been planning to move to Colorado with me.

She was going to enroll in school there to stay with me.

A few days ago, I had thought I had everything figured out and in place, and it was all a fucking lie. That one simple phone call from Frankie had proven that, and now this. I had no damn clue what I was doing anymore.

"Dr. McVaughn is on his way." The trainer walked into the room and pushed past Carson to get to me.

He had a pair of scissors in his hand, and he started cutting my uniform from my leg before I even realized what he was doing. I winced as the metal moved around my knee. My entire lower leg was throbbing.

"Carson, there's a girl out here asking for Olly. She says she's his fiancée," someone said from near the doorway, but I didn't have the energy to look up at who it was.

"Shit. Hold on," Carson called out to them before moving in front of me. "Olly?"

I didn't say a word. I simply shook my head, and he nodded once before walking away. Guilt flooded me because she should have been the exact person I wanted to be with right now, but she wasn't.

The thought alone made me feel bone-tired.

"Here, Olly." Coach put a pillow back on the table

behind me. "Lay back and try to relax. I know it's hard, but try to breathe through the pain."

I did as he said. I laid back against the pillow, and I ran my hands over my face as they tremble. I could hear Carson talking with the locker room door open, but I didn't pay a bit of attention to what he was saying. Instead, I closed my eyes, and I thought about Frankie.

I thought about the way her voice had sounded the last time I talked to her and how she rushed off the phone after she heard me say I love you to Jordan. I drew up the memory of the way her perfume smelled and the way her nose wrinkled when she laughed.

She was the only thing that took my mind off the pain, and for the first time in a long time, I let myself think about her freely. No guilt. No shame. It was just her, and the pain in my chest drowned out everything else.

CHAPTER 14
FRANKIE

I slammed my hand down on my phone as the loud vibrating woke me up. I didn't know who the hell was calling me in the middle of the night, but I had no intentions of answering it.

Ben rolled into my back, and the heat of his body felt like it was covering me like a heavy blanket. It was too much, and I was so damn uncomfortable as I kicked the sheets from around my legs.

It wasn't enough. Everything felt like it was bothering me. His skin against mine, the way my tank top was pulled to the side, the hair on the top of my head.

I slipped out from under his arm and sat up on the side of the bed. It was only midnight which meant I had barely been asleep for an hour, and tomorrow was going to be a long fucking day.

I unplugged my phone from the charger as I stood, and I blinked down at the screen as it lit up Ben's dark bedroom.

One missed call from Olly.

My heart hammered in my chest as I stared down at his

name. How dare he call me now? After everything that had happened.

It had been a little over two weeks since I talked to him, and I hadn't really handled things very well. I had hung up on him before he had gotten a chance to say anything more, but I had thought about it over and over every single day.

The way he had said he loved her felt like it was haunting me.

But what haunted me more was the invitation I had received in the mail today from his mother. I didn't believe it as I stared down at the thick cream invitation that had his name penned in perfect calligraphy at the top.

Why was he calling me now? I had no idea what he could possibly have to say, but I knew that I probably wouldn't be able to handle it.

I pressed my phone against my chest as I tiptoed to the door and slid out of Ben's room. I slowly pulled the door closed behind me and jumped slightly as the loud latch echoed through the space.

What was I doing? I got up in the middle of the night frequently when I stayed the night at Ben's, and I never felt like I had to sneak around. I was being paranoid for no reason, but I knew it was because I had every intention of calling Olly back.

If I didn't, I would regret not knowing what he had to say. I regretted so many things when it came to him.

And that regret only grew when I saw Jordan's name next to his as if it was meant to be there. She was going to become Mrs. Olly Warner, and I felt like I was going to be sick.

When I had first held the invitation in my hand, I hadn't been able to think straight. There were so many emotions running through me: pain, anger, heartbreak, regret.

So many regrets.

That was all I could think about as I dropped the invitation and tried to breath. Olly wasn't mine, and I regretted every single decision that led us to this place.

He was happy and getting everything he wanted, and I was... fuck... I was...

Falling apart.

I reached for the invitation that I had tucked inside my book that was sitting on the coffee table, and I flipped it over in my hand as I sank into the couch.

The invitation was beautiful, and Mr. And Mrs. Warner joyfully invited me to celebrate the engagement of their son. That was what it actually said. Joyfully invited.

They were so damn fake, and I honestly couldn't believe that Olly was letting them host an engagement party at all. But this Olly on the invite wasn't my Olly.

I ran my fingers over the embossed lettering one more time before I clicked his name on my phone and pressed my phone to my ear. My knee bounced against the couch and my heart raced in my chest as I listened to it ring.

He answered quickly, only allowing the phone to ring a few times, and I took a deep breath when I heard his voice.

"Hello?"

"You do realize that it's midnight here, right?" I tossed the invitation down on the couch beside me. "Not all of us are living on California time."

I had no idea what I was saying. I hadn't intended to call him and reprimand him for calling me so late, but I was so damn angry and it was the only thing I could think to say.

"Shit. I'm sorry." His voice was rough, and it did things to my stomach that it shouldn't have. "I wasn't thinking."

"Why are you calling, Olly?" I clenched my hand into a

fist as I stared straight ahead. "I got your invitation. Are you wanting my RSVP? Don't worry. I wouldn't miss it for the world."

"My invitation?" He sounded so confused, and it only made me angrier. I knew that I had no right to be angry at him, but my feelings weren't rational right now.

"How dare you let me find out like this, Olly? You could have picked up the fucking phone and called me. You could have sent me a fucking email. Fuck, I don't know. You could have sent one of our friends." It hit me then and my stomach sank harder. "Oh my God. Everyone else already knew."

"No." Olly rushed to answer me. "Shit. No. Almost no one knows. Carson and Allie do, of course, but I asked him not to say anything until I could talk to you."

That did nothing to make me feel any better. If anything, it just made me feel betrayed by Allie and Carson. But nothing compared to the betrayal I felt from him.

He had done nothing wrong, yet everything about it felt like it was.

"But your mom is already sending out invitations to your engagement party?" I bit down on the side of my thumb as I tried to calm myself down. I could feel the panic rising in my chest and my voice was rising with it. I was going to wake up Ben.

"I swear that I just talked to her about it and agreed to let them host it. I had no idea she was sending out invitations." He groaned. "Fuck, Frankie. I would have never let her... I'm sorry."

"It doesn't matter." I shook my head even though it did. It fucking mattered a lot. "Is that why you're calling me in the middle of the night? To tell me that you're officially off the market? The chance of Olly and Frankie is officially over."

"No." I could hear him shifting through the phone, and I could have sworn I heard a small hiss of pain. "I called you because I just needed to talk to you. I needed to hear your voice."

"I think you meant to dial Jordan's number." I was being cruel, but I couldn't stop. It wasn't fair. I was the one who caused this. I was with Ben, and Olly didn't owe me anything. But why did it feel like he owed me the world? Like I was holding out for him to give it to me, and now I felt cheated.

"Frankie," he whispered my name in a way that made me crave him with a fierceness.

"Don't." I shook my head.

"I'm not going to Colorado."

His words shocked me to the point that I almost dropped my phone. "What? What happened?"

"I tore my ACL tonight." He laughed like there was something funny about him being hurt. "I'm going to need surgery, and I didn't have a contract yet with them."

"They can't do that." I jumped to my feet and paced around the living room. "Are you okay?"

"I'm..." His voice broke, and something inside of me broke with it. "Honestly, I don't have a fucking clue."

"Olly, tell me what to do." My hands trembled, and I looked around Ben's apartment as if I was searching for something that could help me.

"There's nothing you can do."

I imagined him shrugging his shoulders with a soft smile on his face that he thought hid his sadness but didn't.

"I can come there. I can help you." I was looking for my shoes, but I didn't even have pants on.

"Frankie, stop. You're not coming here."

"Why not?"

"Because I'm not your responsibility." He sighed. "Plus, what would Ben say when you dropped everything to go across the country to help an old boyfriend."

"You were never my boyfriend," I pointed out the technicality, and he laughed softly. "And Ben doesn't know anything about our past."

"Ahh." There was another small moan of pain. I knew he was trying to keep it from me so I wouldn't be worried. "Jordan does."

He paused for a long moment, and I didn't dare say a word. I didn't know what he wanted me to say.

"That's why we got engaged. Isn't that ironic?" He chuckled again, and I hated the way it sounded. "She was so upset about the way I still felt about you that she was going to leave. She knew that I was still in love with you, and I needed to prove somehow that I loved her too."

I slammed my eyes shut and pressed my hand against the back of the couch to hold me up. "But you do love her?"

"Do you love Ben?"

"I don't know. I think so." I was honest with him. "But I'm not sure."

"Yeah." I imagined him nodding his head as if he understood exactly how I felt. "I do love Jordan, but it's not the same. It's not like that with you, Frankie."

"Olly."

"Shit, I know." This time the sound of his pain was loud and palpable, and everything inside me begged me to go to him.

"Are you at home? Who's there with you?" I just needed to know that someone was taking care of him.

"Carson's sleeping on the floor in my room." He chuckled. "He's been attached to my side like a little mother hen."

I smiled at the thought, but it also made me nervous. If Carson was taking his injury that seriously, then it was bad. It had to be.

"And Jordan?"

"She's at her apartment. I think I hurt her because I didn't want to see her after it happened. I didn't want to see anyone."

"That's understandable, Olly. You're hurt." And his dreams were being stripped away so easily.

"Yeah. I know." He took a deep breath. "I honestly wouldn't feel guilty at all, but I had wanted you. I was in so much pain, and all I could think about was you."

"You're getting married, Olly," I whispered the reality between us for us both to hear, and I could feel tears welling in my eyes as my chest ached.

"I know." His voice was just as quiet as mine. It was as if neither one of us were ready for it to be real. But he had made it real. "I'm sorry."

"For falling for someone else?" I laughed because that was a ridiculous thing to apologize for. Olly deserved to be happy, and if Jordan made him that way, then I would be happy for him too.

"For everything." He sighed, and my fingers ached with the need to touch him. I felt desperate to feel his skin beneath mine, to touch every inch of him and know that he was okay. "I'm sorry for calling you tonight. This was a dick move, and I shouldn't have put any of this on you."

"I would have been pissed if you didn't call me."

He chuckled. "Yeah. You probably would have been. I'm

sorry you found out about me and Jordan through my mom."

"It's okay, Olly." Nothing was okay.

"No. It's not."

I wanted to scream at him. I wanted to tell him that he was making a mistake and so was I. We were both fucking up so badly, and I didn't know how to fix it.

I wasn't sure that we could.

"Go get some sleep. I shouldn't have woken you."

"Olly."

"I'm good, Frankie. I promise." Another fake laugh. "I should probably get some sleep too. I think tomorrow's going to be a long day."

"Okay." I nodded. "But you'll call me if you need me?"

I didn't know what I could do. I was thousands of miles away from him, but I would do whatever he needed.

"Of course."

"Okay, then."

We were both quiet for a long moment, and I didn't want to hang up the phone. I didn't want to let go because I feared how long it would be before I heard his voice again.

"I love you, Frankie." His voice was so soft that I almost didn't hear him.

"I love you too."

CHAPTER 15
FRANKIE

Two Months Later

I didn't know what I was doing.

My hands trembled as I fumbled with the small handbag in my lap, and I couldn't make them stop. They had been shaking all day as I took extra time to get ready. My hair was perfectly curled, and my dress laid against my body in a way that had felt effortless.

But on the inside, I was a complete and total mess.

I had been for days.

Ben rested his arm against the back of my seat and smiled at me as he drove. He just smiled at me like I wasn't falling apart over someone else. It was ridiculous, really.

We were headed to Olly's engagement party, and I needed to get myself pulled together. I couldn't fall apart there in front of everyone.

Not in front of Olly or Ben or anyone else who was watching.

I had barely spoken to Olly since our last phone call.

Mostly short texts and updates on his knee. He didn't sound like himself even over text, and I hated it. Carson said that he was taking everything hard, and of course, he was.

I couldn't imagine what he was going through, and I didn't want to make anything worse for him.

The one time I had called, Jordan had answered. I could barely breathe as I heard her voice come through the line, but she was nothing but kind to me. She let me know that Olly was resting and that she would let him know that I called to check on him.

I had wanted to ask her what her life was like with him. Did she realize how amazing he was? Did she take for granted the little moments with him like I had?

But I didn't ask her any of that. Instead, I got off the phone as quickly as I could, and I didn't call back.

He hadn't called me either.

So much had changed for him, and I knew that I was the furthest thing from his mind. And that was okay. He had surgery only a few short days after we talked, and he needed to focus on his recovery.

Carson assured me that Olly could still play ball once he was healed, but it would take a long time before he would be ready to get back on the field. When I had asked him about Colorado, Carson had gotten quiet, and I knew that wasn't good.

But here we were now, and I wasn't ready to face him.

We pulled up outside the Warners' massive home, and I looked out the window at all the cars that lined their drive-way. This wasn't a small engagement party meant to cele-brate Olly and Jordan. It was just another opportunity for Olly's parents to show off in front of their friends and colleagues, and my stomach hardened as I stared at the crisp white flowers that lined their entryway.

Ben was already climbing out of the car and making his way to my side, and I quickly closed my eyes and took a shuddering breath while no one was watching.

You can do this, Frankie.

Ben opened my door before reaching his hand out for me, and I let him take it. I stepped out of the car and straightened my baby blue dress against my thighs.

"You ready?"

"Yeah." I wrapped my hand around Ben's arm and clamped my fingers around my small clutch. I wasn't ready at all.

We walked up to the door and were greeted by a man who directed us through the house and out the back. It was midday, and the sun was high in the sky. I slipped my sunglasses over my eyes as I looked around at their extravagant backyard that was decorated in pure elegance and luxury. It looked more like a wedding than an engagement party.

There were several tables covered in crisp white linens and beautiful china, but it was the excess of flowers that really took your breath away. There were arrangements of white and pink and the lightest shade of yellow everywhere you looked.

"There's your brother." Ben pointed to a table near the front of the yard, and I tugged his arm and headed in that direction.

Beck was standing behind Josie with his hands on her chair, and he was laughing at something Carson was saying across from him. Allie was the first person to spot me as we walked up, and I could see the pity in her eyes before either of us uttered a word.

"Hey." I tightened my hand on Ben as we stepped up to the table, and everyone's attention swung to me.

"Hi!" Josie jumped out of her seat and pulled me into a hug. My hand slid from Ben as I wrapped my arms around her and hugged her harder than I should have. I couldn't help it. I missed her even though I wasn't that far away. Our lives were changing, all of them, and it was hitting me now just how much.

"You look beautiful." She pulled me away from her but still held me close to her with her hands on my upper arms. She glanced over at Ben, but he was shaking hands with Carson. "Are you okay?"

"Of course, I am." I smiled at her. "Why wouldn't I be?"

"Frankie."

"Did you all save us a seat?" I stepped out of her touch and pulled out one of the chairs. "Or do I need to go sit with Mom and Dad?"

"Those are yours." Beck rolled his eyes before wrapping his arm around my shoulders. "Have you seen Olly yet?"

"No." I shook my head and dropped my clutch down by my plate. "Not yet."

"Oh. There he is." I looked up just as he said it, and I spotted Olly instantly. He was standing near his parents, and his hand was resting against his thigh. I knew he was in pain. He was barely supposed to be walking yet, let alone standing around at some damn party while people he didn't care about talked his ear off.

The urge to go over there and take him a seat was overwhelming, and I stepped away from my brother with the intention of doing just that. But then I saw her.

Jordan was standing at his side, between him and his mother, and she looked so perfect up there with them.

Her light brown hair was pulled back in an intricate updo at the nape of her neck, and the simple white floor-length dress she wore looked lovely.

I pressed my hand against my stomach as I watched her look up at him with a smile. She looked so in love, and I don't know why that thought hadn't really hit me until that moment. She was really and truly in love with him, and I knew that she was looking at him like I did.

And for some reason, that made this hurt so much worse. I thought I could handle this when I had painted her as the villain in my mind, but she wasn't. She was just another girl who was in love with Olly.

I was as much the villain to her as she was to me.

Someone touched the back of my arm, and I jumped before I realized it was Ben.

"You okay?"

"Yeah." I nodded and pushed some hair behind my ear. I wished everyone would quit asking if I was okay. I could only tell so many lies in one day before I cracked. "We should go congratulate them." I nodded toward where Olly stood as I wrapped my hand back around Ben's arm.

I didn't want to do this. That was all I could think as we walked closer and closer to them. I didn't want to celebrate Olly with someone else. I didn't want to see him look at her and wish that it was me.

But I didn't have a choice.

"Oh, Frankie!" Mrs. Warner saw me approaching before anyone else, and she smiled before stepping forward and wrapping me in a tight hug.

I heard a soft but sharp inhale of breath, and my gaze

met Jordan's before I could think better of it. She was staring directly at me, and I could see the hesitation in her eyes.

I was Olly's past, and she was becoming his future.

"How are you, dear?" Mrs. Warner finally let me go, and I brought my attention back to her. I still hadn't looked at Olly, and I wasn't sure that I could.

"I'm good." I nodded and gave her a small smile.

She looked at me expectantly, and it took me a moment to realize that she was waiting for me to introduce Ben.

"Oh." I turned to him, and he smiled even though it didn't reach his eyes. "Mrs. Warner, this is Ben. Ben, this is Olly's mom and dad, and of course, you know Olly." I finally faced him, and I didn't stand a chance of hiding the emotion I knew they could all see.

He just stared back at me. He stared at me with a look that fucked with my head, and I wanted to scream at him. *What the fuck were we doing, Olly?*

"It's nice to meet you, Ben." Olly's mom was talking, but I could barely hear a word she said.

I was too busy watching him and the way Jordan had just reached out for his hand and laced her fingers with his.

"Have you all had the pleasure of meeting Olly's fiancée, Jordan?"

I blinked and finally pulled my attention away from him. "We met once. A long time ago."

"Did we?" Jordan scrunched her nose and let out a small laugh. "I'm so sorry. I don't remember."

"You did." Olly finally spoke, and his voice was like a warm caress down my spine. "How are you, Frankie?"

"I'm good." I looked back over at him and attempted to smile. I was so damn thankful for the sunglasses because even if I wasn't pulling it off well now, I wouldn't have been able to hide anything from him if he had been able to see my eyes.

I never could.

"I'm so excited for you both. Congratulations."

"Thank you." The response came from Jordan. Olly was too busy watching me, studying me.

"But how are you, Olly?" I let my gaze slide down to his knee that was covered in black slacks. I could see the bulge under the fabric and knew he was wearing some sort of brace. "Shouldn't you be sitting down?"

"I'm perfectly capable of standing on my own," he snapped, his voice hard and unyielding, and my gut sank. Olly was in pain, and it had nothing to do with the physical scars he bared.

"I wasn't insinuating that you weren't." I scrunched my brows as I watched him and that stubborn look on his face. "But maybe if you sat down for a bit, you wouldn't be such an asshole."

There was a shocked gasp, and I wasn't sure if it came from Jordan or his mom, but I didn't care. A smile formed on the corner of Olly's mouth before he let out a laugh.

The pain in my chest eased the tiniest bit as I heard the sound.

"You're probably right." He ran his fingers through his hair and messed with the perfectly coiffed style. It looked so much better that way anyway. "I'm glad you made it, Frankie."

"Me too." I lied to him, but what would one more lie between us hurt? "We'll get out of your way." I reached for Ben even though I had almost forgotten he was there. "You look beautiful, Jordan."

She looked shocked at my words, but she hid it quickly. "Thank you."

I didn't wait for him to say anything else. I simply walked away with Ben's hand in mine, and I stopped when we were almost back at the table. "I'm going to run to the ladies' room." Why did I sound so out of breath?

"Okay." He nodded, and I watched as he looked back at Olly before looking down at me. "Do you want me to go with you or...?"

"No." I shook my head and smiled at him. "Go grab a drink. I'll meet you back at the table."

"Okay," he said the word, but he sounded so hesitant. He was looking down at me like he barely knew me, and I didn't blame him.

But I didn't have time to worry about it either.

I felt like everything was crashing down around me, and I didn't know how to handle it. Hell, I could barely remember how to breathe as I walked away from him and pushed through the maze of tables.

The urge to run was overwhelming. I looked over my shoulder at the beach that lay just beyond the Warners' property, and I felt desperate to be out there. I wanted to escape everyone at this damn party and all the noise and fake hellos.

But I didn't do any of that.

Instead, I walked through the back door and turned left past the kitchen to find the bathroom. There was a young girl dressed in the same white shirt as the servers standing at the beginning of the hallway.

"This bathroom is occupied, but if you'd like..."

I didn't wait to hear the rest of her sentence. I could feel the panic rising in my chest, and I couldn't just stand there and let everyone watch me fall apart.

I walked out into the main foyer and the staircase caught my eye. I gripped the rail in my hand and climbed the stairs two at a time. I fumbled in my heels, but I kept going.

I didn't stop until I stood outside the room that I knew used to belong to Olly, and I pushed inside before I could think better of it. I had only been in his room a handful of times, but it still looked the same as I remembered.

His bed took up most of the space and was perfectly made with a dark blue bedding. The smell of him consumed the space. There were hints of the spicy, expensive cologne he had always worn along with a scent that was uniquely him.

I let myself breathe it in, taking in breath after breath of Olly as I tried to calm the rising panic in my chest. I ran my fingers over the baseball trophies that lined his wooden dresser, and I smiled when I spotted a photograph of him, Carson, and Beck with their arms wrapped around each other.

I walked around his room, and it felt so much like Olly while also not. This room represented a version of him that his parents expected. This was their son Olly's room, but it wasn't my Olly's.

With the exception of the baseball memorabilia, nothing in here looked like him. It was all a front, a perfect little lie, and it hit me then how good he had always been at it. Making everyone happy despite the consequences to him.

He had done it with his parents, he had done it with Beck, and I knew that he had done it with me as well.

Olly had hurt me, but I had hurt him so much more. I had pushed him away when it was the last thing either of us really wanted, but he had accepted it. He respected what I was doing to us because he thought that was what I wanted.

But now I had no idea.

I didn't know how to make him see the truth behind all the lies I had been telling myself and him. I didn't know how to move on and let him be happy with Jordan when he looked so miserable at her side.

I was selfish, and I had been that way for a long time.

I sat down on his bed and ran my fingers over the soft fabric. The color was in perfect contrast to my dress, so dark to my light, but they still looked so beautiful together.

I lifted one of the pillows in my hands, and I pressed it to my nose and inhaled deeply. It had clearly been laundered since Olly last slept in here, but it still held the scent of him deep in the fibers.

It reminded me of his t-shirt that was still hidden in the back of my closet. It didn't matter how many times I had washed it. It held on to him as hard as I had.

My forehead fell against the pillow, and I wrapped my arms around it as I held it against me. I could do this. I could pull myself together and be happy for Olly if this was what he wanted.

I had no choice but to do so.

He had told me that he loved her even if he had said he loved me too. We were here to celebrate their engagement, the promise he gave her, and that was the decision he had made.

A decision I had pushed him to.

But none of that seemed to matter as I pressed my eyes closed and begged the tears not to flow.

I could remember every moment that I had ever spent with Olly, every last touch and smile, but they were just that.

Memories.

We were a memory that neither one of us had been willing to let go of, and I still wasn't sure that I could. Even if I wanted to, the ghost of who we had been was always there. I was haunted by the greatest love I had ever known, and I clung to that reminder of who I had been then like a lifeline.

I didn't know who I would become without Olly. Even with the time we had been apart, I had always felt like I still belonged to him, and I didn't know how to be anything else.

I didn't want to be anyone else's.

Not even Ben's.

And that made me more selfish than anything else.

Tears leaked from the corners of my eyes and streamed down my face. A soft sob escaped my throat as I tried to catch my breath, but it was useless.

Coming here and trying to pretend like I wasn't still madly in love with Olly had been futile.

The handle to his bedroom door rattled, and I jumped up from his bed so quickly that I almost fell over in my heels. I still held his pillow against my chest as I turned to face the door, and I squeezed it tighter against me as I saw him standing there.

Olly pushed through the door before quickly closing it behind him, and his frantic gaze searched every inch of me. "What are you doing up here?"

I opened my mouth to answer him, but not a single sound came out. I couldn't think, let alone talk about what was racing through my mind. Especially not when he was standing there looking so fucking handsome, and I couldn't even touch him.

He was so damn close to me, yet he was so far away.

It felt like that was what we would always be destined for.

"Frankie." He took a step toward me, and I took a step back.

"I just needed a minute."

"A minute for what?" He searched my face, and I knew that he could see right through me without me saying a word.

I simply shrugged my shoulders and held on to his pillow. His gaze dropped there before he ran his fingers over the back of his neck, and he looked so conflicted.

"Go back downstairs, Olly," I whispered and looked out his bedroom window. I could see the party still in full swing below, and I knew that everyone was probably looking for the man of honor.

He took another step closer to me, and I wished that he would stop. We both had people downstairs that we were meant to be loyal to, but I wasn't strong enough.

Whatever Olly asked of me, I would give him.

He didn't stop, though. Not until he was right in front of me and had ripped the pillow from my arms. He tossed it onto his bed and looked down at me.

He lifted his right hand and pressed it against my jaw. I could feel him trembling, and I was a fool for ever thinking that I was capable of not having him in my life.

That one simple touch did more to me than anything Ben had ever done, and I couldn't force the guilt to come. It felt too damn good to have his skin on mine, and the pull deep in my gut was from longing and nothing else.

"You look gorgeous." His thumb ran over my cheek, and he skimmed just under my eye where tears had fallen only moments before. "You always do."

"Go downstairs," I begged of him and gripped his wrist in my hand. "Please, Olly." There was so much panic in my voice. "Please walk away from me."

"What if I don't want to?" His words were whispered and dangerous. Everything about him being up here with me right now was risky.

I was constantly risking my heart every time I was near him.

"You don't really have a choice, Olly." I looked at the door behind him. "Everyone is waiting for you down there."

"I wish everyone would quit telling me what I'm allowed to choose."

My gaze snapped up to meet his.

"I've been trying to choose you since what feels like forever."

My chest ached from the speed of my heart hammering against it. I didn't know what to say to him.

"And I think that I owe it to you to make that choice despite what anyone else thinks."

"You are getting married, Olly," I whispered our reality because it wasn't something I wanted to be real. I wished that we could take it all back and go back to who we were before we let the world in.

Everything had felt perfect then, but this was a mess.

We didn't get to make easy decisions about whether we wanted to be together or not. People would be hurt, and my chest ached harder as I thought about Ben waiting for me downstairs.

"I don't want to marry Jordan."

My eyes slammed closed. Everything about this was torture. He was saying things that I had been dying inside to hear, but there was still a party in full swing downstairs to celebrate his love with someone else.

"I need to go back downstairs to Ben." I took a step away from Olly, but he caught my wrist in his hand before I could fully get away.

"Don't, Frankie."

I jerked my hand from his and turned to fully face him. "You choosing me is going to hurt her." I took another step back toward the door. "We haven't seen each other in forever, and seeing me today, it's messing with your head. But we can't do this today. Not like this."

"That's bullshit, and you know it."

"You scare me." I was honest with him for what felt like the first time in a very long time. "I have never felt with anyone what I feel for you, and it's scares me. You can choose me, but then rip it away like you were never mine."

"Frankie."

"I can't handle losing you twice, Olly." I shook my head as I tried to make sense of all the thoughts running through my head. "If this is what you want, then you have to be sure. I can't do this simply because you're having doubts. You have to be sure about me."

He reached out for me again, but I didn't dare let him touch me again. Instead, I pushed from his room as fast as my feet would carry me. Tears were welling in my eyes as I rushed down the stairs, and I took a deep breath and tried to pull myself together.

Ben would know something was wrong. He wasn't Olly, but he still knew me. He knew the version of me that I allowed him to, and he knew her enough to know that I was upset.

I couldn't fathom the thought of him knowing that I was

this fucking destroyed over a man I had barely seen over the last few years. I had been at his side, in his bed, and the entire time, I had been thinking about Olly.

And that was so damn foolish.

I could hear Olly coming down the stairs behind me, but I didn't stop or turn around. I kept pushing through the house in search of Ben.

We couldn't do this today. Ben would be hurt. Jordan would be crushed.

I pushed out into the backyard and dropped my sunglasses back down on my face. I didn't smile at anyone as I passed. I just pushed through all of them in search of something that I could hold on to. I was hunting for anything that I could grasp in my fingers and wouldn't slip away.

I passed by my parents' table, and my mom called my name, but I didn't stop. I couldn't. I just needed something. Anything.

I felt desperate. Panicked.

I needed to...

I was jerked to a stop when someone caught my hand in theirs, and I gasped before spinning around. Olly stood behind me, and he gripped his leg as he winced in pain.

"Would you please fucking stop?" His voice was loud, and a hush rippled through the crowd of people around us.

"Let me go." I jerked my hand from his, but he didn't budge. He gripped me so tightly that I knew I would never get away unless he wanted me to.

"No." He shook his head, and I could see the frustration on his face.

"Olly." I pulled my gaze away from him long enough to see everyone staring at us, and I caught his mom and Jordan making their way toward us through the corner of my eye. "Olly, let me go right now."

"I fucking said no, Frankie. I need you to listen to me."

I shook my head before whispering, "This isn't the time or the place."

"It never seems to be the time or the place, and I'm tired of us fucking running from each other because we're fucking scared."

"What's going on?" His mom's voice rushed out as she finally made her way over to us and put her hand on Olly's shoulder. He didn't pay her a bit of attention. His attention was still solely focused on me.

"Frankie." I heard Ben's voice behind me, and I winced as I turned to him.

But Olly caught my chin in his hand before I could completely turn away. "Please stop running."

"Olly, what are you doing?"

Olly finally pulled his attention away from me long enough to look at his mother, and I felt it the exact moment his gaze connected with Jordan's. He didn't let me go. Instead, his hands tightened on me as if he was using those exact spots we were connected for strength.

"I can't do this," he said it so softly, but Jordan jerked back as if he had hit her.

"What?" His mom's voice was shrill, but no one was paying any attention to her.

I tried to pull away from him again, but he still wouldn't let me go. "Olly, don't do this to her."

He finally looked down at me, and I tried to swallow around my emotion. He finally let his hands drop from me, and I sagged backward as if he had been my gravity.

I knew that he always had been. Olly was always the one

thing that was pulling me, altering my decisions, even when I was doing it subconsciously.

"Jordan, can we talk?"

Jordan took the smallest step back, and I could see the heartbreak in her eyes. She already knew without him saying anything. "You're choosing her?" She pressed her hand to her chest just as a man I didn't recognize stepped up behind her.

He wrapped his arm around her, and the way she looked up at him before looking back at Olly, I knew it was her father.

"Let's go inside and talk."

"No." She shook her head and a small laugh escaped her. "I knew that you were still in love with her. I knew, but..." She looked at me then, and there was so much venom in her eyes. "Are you happy?"

"I didn't..."

"Leave Frankie out of it."

"Leave her out of it," she yelled and swung her attention back to him. "How could I leave the girl out of it when she's been a part of our relationship from the very beginning?" She shook her head, and her hand fisted at her side. "Do you think I don't know about her picture that you have hidden inside your wallet or the way you always turn to her when something really bad is happening in your life?"

Someone pressed against my back, and I flinched before looking over my shoulder at Ben. Except Ben was no longer there. It was Beck who stood at my back, and I sagged against him and allowed him to support me.

Beck was the one who had started this mess. He was the one who hadn't approved of us, but he wasn't responsible for where we were. That blame was completely on me and Olly and us alone.

"I don't know what..."

"It's not your fault, Olly." Jordan shook her head. "You warned me a long time ago that you were still in love with her, and I should have listened to you." She glanced back toward me. "I thought that I could love him enough to make him forget you, but I was wrong."

I didn't say anything back. I didn't know what I could say that would do anything to help take away the anger or the hurt that I could see coursing through her.

"How dare you?" This came from Olly's mom, and when I looked at her, she was staring straight at me. "How fucking dare you?"

"Don't fucking talk to her that way." Beck's chest rumbled against my back.

"He is engaged, Frankie." His mom pointed toward Jordan. "How dare you interfere with what he wants?"

Both Beck and Olly started talking, but all I could hear was the roaring in my head and the words that escaped past my lips. "You don't have a damn clue what he wants. You never have." I straightened my shoulders. "You parade him around like he's a fucking show pony, but he's not. He is your son."

I pointed to Olly, and I could feel my anger rising and rising.

"You punish him for following his dreams. You act like he's not good enough because he doesn't want to be a cookie cutter of you and his father. When was the last time you asked him what he wanted, Mrs. Warner?"

She blinked up at me but didn't say a word.

"When he hurt his knee, were you concerned or were

you celebrating that he was no longer going to be able to follow his dream?"

"That's enough," she demanded, and she was right. I had gone too far, but I couldn't bring myself to care.

I attempted to step back from all of them, but my back was still pressed against Beck.

"What do you think is going to happen here, Frankie? Do you think he's going to come back home and be with you simply because he saw you again and you confused him?"

I knew that she was wrong, but at the same time, she had hit my biggest fear. I didn't want Olly to want me simply because he didn't know what he wanted. I didn't want to be his crutch that he would regret.

"That's up to them." My brother's words shocked me. "If Frankie and Olly want to be together, then that is up to them and nobody else."

"I beg to fucking differ," Jordan's dad finally piped in. "We came all the way from California to celebrate your engagement, and what? You're going to ruin everything because you caught a glimpse of your old whore?"

I winced because he shouldn't have said that, but he wasn't wrong in his anger. I would be furious too.

But I didn't get a chance to respond. Olly surged forward and slammed his fist into his face and almost knocked into Jordan. Beck jumped forward and reached out for Olly before he could do anything more and pulled him back against him.

I saw Olly grimace hard as he took a step back on his bad leg, but he pushed the pain away as he pointed toward Jordan's dad. "Don't you ever fucking talk about her like that again."

I was tugged backward, and I turned to look back at

Josie. "I think we should go." She nodded toward the house. "Ben just stormed toward the front of the house."

I nodded my head but glanced back at Olly. He was looking at me too. There was panic in his eyes, but I didn't know how to take it away. I didn't know how to fix all the things that we had fucked up so badly.

Especially not here and now. He needed to talk to Jordan and decide what he wanted, and he needed to do it alone.

He couldn't make a real decision with me standing here at his side. Even if I was what he thought he wanted, I didn't want to be a rash decision he made out of fear.

I let Josie take my hand in hers and pull me away from them. Everyone at the party was watching what was happening, and I got more than a few dirty looks as Josie weaved me through the crowd.

We pushed through the house, and I could barely keep up with her as she kept going forward.

"Wait." I pulled her to a stop, and she spun around to look at me. "I don't know what I'm doing."

"We're going home, Frankie." She pushed some hair out of my face. "You don't need to be here with all this."

"What about Olly?"

"What about him?" she asked gently. "What are you two doing?"

"I don't know." I shook my head because I didn't have a damn clue.

"Do you want to be with Olly?" She asked the question like it was so simple, and in reality, it was.

"Yes. I always have."

"Then you need to talk to Ben." She looked behind her to the front door, but he was nowhere to be seen. "And Olly needs to figure his shit out."

"You're right." I knew she was, but I still couldn't get my feet to move forward. I was so worried that if I left, he would change his mind. I feared that I would leave this house, and he was going to come to his senses. "What if he chooses her?" My voice cracked, and Josie looked at me with so much pity.

"He won't." She shook her head before pulling me forward, and I finally took a step.

One after another I followed her footsteps until we walked out the front door and into their expansive driveway. She was right. I couldn't stay here and beg him to love me. If he did so, he was going to have to do it all on his own.

And deep down, I knew that he did.

Ben was still standing by his car with his head bowed and his hand on the back of his neck as we stepped outside, and my chest felt like it was caving in on itself.

Despite everything, I did love Ben. It just wasn't the same way that I loved Olly. It wasn't enough.

And I felt so guilty.

Things would have been so much easier if I had been able to force myself to feel for him the way I always had about Olly. He didn't deserve the fact that I didn't.

"Ben." I stepped up to the side of his car, and he slowly raised his head to look up at me.

He looked so damn defeated. "Are you sleeping with him?"

"No." I shook my head and took another step forward. "It's been a long time since Olly and I have been together."

"How long exactly?" His jaw tensed and my stomach dropped.

"Not since the weekend you first came to Clermont Bay."

Ben laughed but there wasn't an ounce of humor. "So,

when I celebrate our anniversary, you're really just cele-brating the last time you fucked the guy you're still in love with?"

I jerked back at his words but didn't answer him. He had every right to be angry.

"Is he why you don't want to move in with me? Why you can barely make plans a few days ahead? Have you been holding out for him all this time?"

"It's not that simple." I shook my head, but God, he was right. He was so fucking right about it all.

"It looks pretty damn simple to me, Frankie. I cannot believe this." He pushed off his car and turned to fully face me. He was looking down at me like he barely knew me, and he was right.

The girl he knew and the girl I was were hardly the same. Each version of myself always had some part of me missing. I was only ever really myself with Olly, and I missed her.

"I can't believe that I decided to stay here for you." He chuckled again. "My mom was right about you."

That jab hurt, but I deserved it. "I didn't mean to hurt you, Ben. I didn't mean for any of this to happen."

He shook his head as if he didn't believe a word I was saying. "But you're still in love with him?"

"I am." I took a step closer to him and tried to calm my racing heart. "We don't get to pick who we fall for, Ben."

"No. We certainly do not." He looked away from me and put his hand on the hood of his car. "Do you love me at all?"

"Yes," I said as tears started to fall from my face. "Of course, I do."

"Just not as much as him." He looked back at me, and I knew that my answer would crush him. But he deserved to know the truth. No matter how badly I didn't want to tell it.

"I have loved Olly for a very long time, Ben." I wrapped my arms around my chest. "I have tried to let him go. I was trying with you. I didn't do anything..."

God, I had tried, but it was never enough.

"You deserve each other, Frankie." He opened his car door before looking back at me. I couldn't stand the pain in his eyes that was staring back at me. Pain that I had caused. "I'll have someone drop off your things at your apartment."

Then Ben climbed into his car and left.

CHAPTER 16
OLLY

My knee was throbbing in pain, but I didn't care.

Josie said that Frankie had gone out to the beach, and I was frantic to find her. I hadn't planned on things happening the way they had.

This morning I was engaged to be married, and now? Now I was searching for the girl that I felt like I had loved half my life. I had no idea how she was feeling or what she wanted, but I knew that I couldn't handle another second without talking to her.

I had to tell her how I felt. She had to know that I called off the engagement with Jordan.

Whether Frankie wanted me or not wasn't important because I was choosing her, and I was going to continue to choose her. Even if she decided that she wanted to stay with Ben and tell me to fuck off.

I was still going to choose her.

And I couldn't bring myself to care what anyone else thought. I had been a coward the first time I walked away from her, and I had allowed her to push me away due to her own fear, but I wasn't willing to do it again.

I was scared to death that she wasn't going to choose me back, but that choice was hers and hers alone.

That was what I had told her brother and everyone else who had tried to stop me from coming out on this beach. They had told me to give her time, but they didn't have a clue. They had no idea that all we had done was give each other time over and over again until we had driven ourselves crazy.

I was tired of time away from her.

I couldn't handle another moment of it.

I spotted her about a mile down the beach from her parents' house, and I pushed through the sand with a bite of pain in my knee with every step.

I had thought I felt pain when everything happened with my knee, but nothing had compared. When I saw Frankie's face at the party today, I knew that nothing would ever hurt that much again. She smiled at me even though she was devastated, and I knew that I couldn't go through with it.

Regardless of if she was in love with someone else, I couldn't force myself to do the same when I looked at her. What I felt for Jordan had never compared.

And I felt like shit for hurting her. That had never been my intention. I had been so focused on not craving Frankie every second of the day, that I had never considered that I would hurt Jordan in the same way.

Not until things had already gotten too far.

I had hurt her, and I never should have. I never should have let her fall in love with me when I was still so wrapped up in someone else.

Frankie didn't hear me until I was almost right behind

her, and I watched as she ran her fingers back and forth through the wet sand. She was still in the blue dress that she had worn to the party, but it was damp now from the ocean rushing up and kissing her legs.

"I should have known I would find you out here." I groaned as I straightened out my leg and dropped to the sand beside her.

Her head jerked in my direction and her dark eyes got so round as she reached out and tried to help me. "What are you doing out here? The sand isn't good for your knee."

"I'm aware." I rubbed the top of my thigh where it was starting to throb with a heavy thrum. "But I had to see you."

There was so much emotion in her eyes as she stared at me, and I hated when she quickly looked away and back out to the ocean. Her safe place.

"I barely come out here anymore." Her fingers trailed through the sand again.

"How come?"

She shrugged her shoulders. "It just hasn't felt right."

I knew exactly what she meant. Nothing felt right anymore.

"Why'd you come out here now?"

"I don't know." She lifted some sand in her fingers and tossed it. It disappeared with the retreating wave, and she looked so mesmerized as she watched it. "I needed to clear my head, and I just ended up here."

"Frankie, I'm sorry about what happened."

"Don't." She held up her hand. Wet sand still stuck to her tan fingers. "You don't have to say anything, Olly. Jordan is your fiancée, and I am... I'm your past."

"You have never been my past."

She finally looked back at me.

"And I'm not apologizing because she's my fiancée. I'm apologizing because she never should have been. I'm trying to say I'm sorry for ever thinking that I could do any of this without you."

She lifted her hand and chewed on the side of her thumb as she watched me.

"I'm sorry that I ever made you think that you weren't worth losing everyone else in this world over. I will lose them all for you, Frankie. I'm willing to give up everything."

"Olly." She shook her head, and I already knew what she was thinking.

"Loving you is not a sacrifice, Frankie. It is a fucking privilege, and I was just too much of a coward to see that before. Your brother was a coward. Nothing is as important as you. Not a single fucking thing."

I swallowed hard when she didn't say anything back.

"You don't have to say anything. I'm not telling you all of this because I expect you to just drop your life and be with me. I know that you have Ben, and you are more than capable of living without me. But I'm not capable of being without you. I will love you either way."

She pushed to her knees, and I wasn't prepared when her chest knocked into mine. She didn't give me time to finish my sentence. She didn't let me finish telling her all the things that I had been desperate to say.

Her mouth hit mine in a rush, and I wrapped my arms around her and crushed her against me. She settled between my thighs, and I winced as her body knocked into my knee.

She noticed. Of course, she did, and she tried to pull away from me.

"I'm so sorry."

I gripped the back of her head and pulled her back against me. "I don't give a fuck about my leg. Kiss me."

She hesitated for the smallest second before her mouth hit mine again, and I fell into the kiss like I had finally found where I belonged after all this time. Frankie was my home, and I wanted to kiss every part of her. I was desperate to taste every bit of hurt I had caused her and not stop until it faded into a memory.

I wanted to graze the wildest parts of her, the parts that I knew she hid from everyone else.

I wanted to soak in everything she was, and I didn't want to stop until she was the only thing I knew.

Everything about us felt chaotic as we pulled at each other's hair and kissed with our lips and tongue and teeth. It was chaos, but it was real. We always had been.

I lost control when I was with her. Control over my perspective, over the ability to protect myself.

But she was the most beautiful kind of madness. She was a thunderstorm, loud and passionate and so fucking destructive, but on the days when the rain disappeared, I missed her even harder.

She had wrecked me for anyone else, but I didn't want it any other way.

I wanted to give her the world, but I knew that I wasn't capable of that. Instead, I would give her everything I had.

I pulled her hair at the base of her neck and pulled her mouth away from mine. I needed her to hear me. I was frantic for her to know.

"I love you, Frankie."

A small sob passed her lips and her fingers dug into my skin as if she was trying to make up for a thousand years of not touching me. "I love you too."

"I feel like I'm starving for you." I ran my hand down her neck and watched as she gasped down a breath over and over again.

"I know." She groaned out the word and pushed closer to me.

"I need to taste you, to be inside of you. I fucking crave you." My hands pressed into her hips, and I held her until I knew she felt the bite of pain from my fingers. But I couldn't stop.

I wanted to unravel every inch of her.

"I'm yours, Olly. I always have been."

I lifted her up until her legs were straddling mine and her dress rose high up on her hips.

"And I'm yours." I ran my hand up her body, over her breast, and against her heart. I had barely touched her and already I was drowning in everything that she was.

Her chest trembled beneath my touch, and I realized that every part of her was. She pushed her hips down against mine and rocked into me with a soft whimper.

The sound was fucking magic, her want putting me under a spell. I caressed my fingers down every inch of her skin just like I had in my dreams. She spread her legs farther, and I didn't stop.

I touched every part of her that I planned on consuming. I whispered promises of what was to come with my fingers before slowly following with my mouth, and it infuriated me that I had gone so long without this.

I was jealous of my own touch. I was jealous of the sun as it kissed her skin in places I had yet to get to.

My fingers dug into her thighs, and I spread them farther as I watched. She was pressed against me, and her pussy was covered in the thinnest white lace.

I could see the wetness there, her want for me bleeding through the fabric, and I felt like I was going mad.

I had never wanted someone so badly in all my life.

It didn't matter that I had her before. Nothing mattered but this moment in front of us, and a chill ran down my spine as I let my fingers trace over the lace.

"Oh God, Olly." She tightened her hands on my shoulders, and I pushed harder against her.

I let my fingers slide beneath the fabric and groaned as my fingers slipped through the moisture. She was so fucking wet, and it was so damn sexy.

I brought my hand from her pussy and slid my middle two fingers into my mouth. God, she tasted so good.

I stared into her eyes as I sucked every bit of her from my fingers, and she bit down on her bottom lip as she watched.

"I've fucking missed this." I sank my hand back into her panties, and I gave her no warning as I pressed hard against her clit. She surged forward and her chest hit mine, but I didn't stop. I rubbed small, calculated circles against her clit as she shook against me.

She was so reactive, so ready to fall apart already, and I knew that she had been as desperate for me as I was for her. There were no pretenses between us, no hiding how badly we wanted one another, and nothing had ever turned me on more.

I never wanted her to hide any part of herself from me. I wanted every bit of her. I wanted to love everything she hated about herself. I wanted to fuck those thoughts away from her with my tongue until she saw how perfect she was.

"I want to fall to my fucking knees before you, Frankie. I want to worship every bit of your body until you have no doubts that it's always been you."

"Your knee is hurt." She pointed out but was still rocking against me.

"I know." I nodded and leaned forward to run my lips over her collarbone. "So, you're going to have to sit on my face and let me fuck you with my mouth."

I leaned back into the sand, and she pressed her hands down on my chest.

"Olly, we are on the beach."

"As if that matters." I wrapped my hands around her thighs and jerked her forward until her ass was pressed against my ribs. "This sand has held so many of our dirty secrets, and it would be cruel to not allow it to see me love you so openly. I don't care who's watching, Frankie. They all need to know that you're mine."

"Oh, God," she whimpered, and I pulled her up higher until her thighs were straddling my head.

I wrapped my arms around each of her thighs and forced them farther apart before I reached for the lace and pulled it out of my way. I looked up at her above me, and she was so goddamn beautiful. My breath caught in my chest as I watched her looking down at me.

I didn't look away from her as I lifted my head from the sand and ran my tongue through her pussy. She took in a sharp breath, and I went harder. I tasted every inch of her before I sucked her clit into my mouth and her chest heaved forward as her legs started to shake in my hands.

My fingers were bruising her as I held her against me, but I couldn't get enough. She was holding herself up just above my mouth, and I ran my teeth gently over her clit until she jerked against my mouth.

"I told you to sit on my face, Frankie." I pulled harder

with my hands until she was forced lower against me. "I want to feel the weight of you on my tongue."

I kept her pinned against my face as I ate her, and I didn't stop until she was riding me and silently begging me for more. I gave it to her.

I sucked and licked and bit down against her until she threw her head back and pressed her hands against my chest behind her. I wanted to love her slowly, but it was impossible. I felt like I was racing to reacquaint myself with every inch of her, and nothing was going to stop me until her soul remembered exactly who I was.

"Fuck, Olly," she cried out and rode me harder.

She looked like a piece of art falling apart above me, and I soaked in every bit of her as she came against my mouth.

"I need to be inside you." I pressed a gentle kiss to the inside of her thighs, and I could have spent all day there making love to her skin. I gripped her ass in my hands and pulled her back against my chest, and I didn't stop until her hips were settled against mine.

I sat up and ran the back of my hand against my mouth and licked the taste of her off my lips.

"We should get you off the beach, Olly. Your leg." She ran her fingers over my hair before streaming them down the back of my neck.

"I don't give a fuck about my leg." I pulled her closer to me and kissed her again. This time, the taste of her was mixed between us, and only turned me on more. She eagerly kissed me, her tongue chasing the traces of her cum that still clung to mine, and I buried my hand in her hair.

I pulled her away from me long enough to move my mouth down her jaw and along her neck.

"Please, Olly." She rolled her hips against mine, and I knew she could feel how hard I was beneath her.

"Tell me what you want." I reached between us and unfastened my belt before popping the button on my slacks. She lifted off me just enough for me to pull my zipper down and pull my cock from my pants. Precum coated the tip, and I pressed my thumb against it before rubbing the moisture against her panties. She flinched as my thumb hit her clit, and her eyes began to flutter shut. "I need you to fucking say it, Frankie."

"You." She opened her eyes, and the darkest shade of brown stared down at me. "I've always wanted you."

My heart hammered in my chest as I slid my cock against her. She was still lifted onto her knees, and her wet pussy felt like it might kill me.

"I've always wanted you too." I looked up at her, and I hoped she realized how serious I was. Intense jealousy hit me as I thought about her being with anyone else. Of course, I knew she had been with Ben, but I had no idea if there had been any others. And I didn't deserve to know.

I had forced her to love someone else, and she had forced me.

But it didn't matter.

Nothing did when it came to her.

"It has always been you, Frankie." I ran my cock against her again, and she moaned as the head pressed against her clit. "It could only ever be you."

Her hands tightened on my shoulders, and she pushed down against me when I pushed the head of my cock at her opening.

"I thought about you." She lowered herself, and I groaned against her chest as I sank inside her.

"I thought about you too." I wrapped my arms around her back as she sat down fully against me. "I couldn't get off without thinking about you." I shook my head against her. "My body nor my heart have ever been able to accept that you weren't mine."

"I am yours." She rocked against me, and I thrust up inside her.

"And I am yours, Frankie. I will always be yours." I rolled my hips beneath her as I tightened my hands against her and lifted her before slamming her back down against me.

I buried my face in her neck as I fucked her, and she clung to me just as tightly. We were both so desperate for each other, but we were also scared to death. Scared of losing each other, scared of losing this feeling.

I had been scared of losing Frankie for so long that I had almost lost her completely. She was my friend, but she was so much more than that. I was a fool for ever thinking we could be something different.

Something less.

Frankie was all-consuming, and I wanted to lose myself in her completely. I didn't give a shit about the consequences anymore. Nothing mattered more to me than her. It never had, but I had been too stupid to realize it.

I had been searching for something more, something that I didn't know I needed, and I hadn't realized that she was the only one who could give it to me.

Frankie was my family. She was my home, and I would never walk away from her again.

She was the only one who had the power to take this away from me, and even then, I would fight for us. I would fight for us in a way that I should have been fighting all along.

There wasn't an inch of room between us, but neither one of us was willing to allow it. I just slammed her down against me as I rolled my hips against her, and only when I felt her thighs tighten against mine did I finally let her go.

I pressed my hand against her chest and pushed her back until she was forced to reach behind her for support. Her hand pressed against my shin on my good leg, but she was careful not to touch the other.

Instead, she rolled her breast in her hand as she stared at me. I wrapped one hand around her neck gently, holding her in place before I pressed my thumb back against her pussy. I rubbed small circles there, and she chased the feeling with her hips.

My stomach tightened, and there was a deep ache low in my back. I was going to come hard, but I refused to get there without her.

She was going to come again, and she was going to do it with me inside her. I needed to feel her tighten around me. I was desperate to feel her fall apart and know that it was me who caused it.

I never wanted her to look at anyone else the way she was looking at me. I was selfish and possessive, but God, I was in love.

I was truly and irrevocably in love with this girl.

She was my weakness and my strength. It was pathetic, really, how in love I was with her. The world could crumble around us right now, and I wouldn't blink. I would still be looking at her just as she was. Like she was the only thing that mattered.

"Olly," she whispered my name and let her head fall back. Her hips moved faster, and her ragged breaths rushed out of her chest.

"I've got you, baby." I thrust up into her as I continued to slam her down against me. Her pussy clamped down around me as she closed her eyes. "Look at me, Frankie. I need your fucking eyes."

She did so immediately before her entire body tightened and her orgasm rolled through her. I followed right behind her. My body was unable to hold on any longer as she came around me, and I slammed inside her as I came. My hands tightened against her, and I refused to let go.

Not now. Not ever.

CHAPTER 17
FRANKIE

We walked hand in hand through the back of my parents' gate, and my heart raced. It wasn't because I was worried or anxious. It was because everything about this felt right.

I didn't know what was going to happen between us or how we were going to make this work, but I knew that we would figure it out. After everything we had been through and how much we had hurt each other, it was going to be me and him.

And that was enough.

I tightened my hand in Olly's as we made our way around the pool and saw my brother sitting in one of the lounge chairs with his head in his hands. Olly lifted my hand to his mouth and kissed my knuckles before tugging me forward.

He didn't drop it as we walked up to Beck and stopped only a few feet away. If anything, his grip on me tightened.

It was quiet for a long moment before Beck finally glanced up and looked back and forth between the two of us.

"I need to…" Beck started, but Olly shook his head.

"Before anyone says anything, I just need to tell you all that I'm in love with Frankie." His hand tightened around mine, and I bit down on the inside of my bottom lip as I stared ahead at my brother. "I have been for a very long time, and it doesn't matter what any of you think." He tugged me closer to him, and I pressed into his side. "I would love your blessing, but I don't fucking need it. You fucked this up for us once, and then we continued to fuck it up from there. But I don't care. I'm going to love her regardless of what you say."

"Okay." Beck nodded before running his hands over his pants.

"What?" I wrinkled my brow and stared at my brother as he stood.

"I said okay," he sighed before his gaze bounced back and forth between me and Olly. "I was wrong. I've been wrong for a very long time because I thought I knew how to protect you better than anyone else." His eyes softened as his gaze ran over me. "I have felt the overwhelming need to protect you from anything and everything that I could, and in doing that, I hurt you. I hurt both of you."

I didn't know what to say. He had hurt me, he hurt both of us, and if he hadn't been so adamant about us being apart, who knows where we would have been. But even as fucked up as it was, I knew that everything Beck had ever done for me was out of love. Even when it was completely wrong.

"And if the two of you have loved each other through everything, I'm not going to stand in your way. Not anymore. I'm sorry that I ever did."

Olly looked down at me as if he was waiting for me to make a decision on what to say or what to do, and I loved him for that. Because I didn't need any more knights in shining armor. I just needed him to be at my side, and he knew that.

I let go of Olly's hand as I stepped forward, and overwhelming emotion hit me as I fell into my brother and wrapped my arms around him. He held me tightly against him as he let out a deep breath against my shoulder, and God, I was so thankful for him. Even if he didn't get things right all the time, I was so blessed to have a brother who wanted to.

"I'm sorry that I was an ass, Frankie," he said only loud enough for me to hear, and I squeezed him closer against me.

"I forgive you, but I don't need you to protect me anymore. I am capable of taking care of myself."

"I know you are." He nodded against me and held me like that for a long moment before he let me go and ran his fingers through his hair. "Mom and Dad want to talk to Olly."

"About what?"

"My guess would be you." He chuckled, and I tensed. They were almost as protective as he was, and I didn't want to hear another word about us not being together.

"Okay." Olly nodded before stepping forward and clapping hands with Beck. They did that weird man hug thing before they pulled apart, but something passed between them as they looked at each other that I would never be privy to. It was as if they had an entire conversation with one simple look. "Your parents inside?"

"Yeah. They're in the kitchen." Beck nodded.

"I'm going with you." I grabbed Olly's hand as he started walking in their direction, and he looked down at me with a smirk.

"I can handle your parents, Frankie."

"I don't care." I didn't. I wasn't letting him go. I clung to him as we pushed through the back door and found my parents sitting at the kitchen table sharing a piece of cake.

"It's about time you two got back," my dad grumbled before my mom smacked him in the chest. "Ow. What was that for?"

"Are you two okay?" My mom ignored my dad and smiled up at us.

"Yeah." I nodded and clung to Olly harder. "We're okay."

"Well, son." My dad pulled out the seat beside him and Olly took it before pulling me down in the seat next to him. "I was hoping we could have this conversation alone, but since it looks like Frankie isn't going to leave your side, we'll just have to do it in front of her."

"Okay." Olly nodded his head, and I could tell he was nervous about whatever my father had to say even though he would never admit it.

"You in love with my girl?" My dad just laid it all out there.

"Dad!"

"I am."

"And what about your knee? Are you still going to play baseball or are you coming home?"

"I honestly don't think there's much left for me in baseball, sir." Olly's voice changed as he admitted that, and I hated it. I hated how everything he had worked so hard for had been ripped away so easily. "I talked to my dad about coming home and working for him."

My dad nodded, and I could see the contemplation in his eyes. "Olly, I know I'm not your father, but you feel like a son to me. You have for a very long time." My dad swallowed, and I could feel emotion clouding my own throat. "I couldn't imagine a better man for my daughter to be in love with even if the two of you have gone the long way around with this whole thing."

My mom said his name under her breath, and my dad rolled his eyes.

"Well, it's the truth. These two have been making goo-goo eyes at each other for as long as I can remember."

I snorted out a laugh, but my dad kept going.

"I know that you don't want to work for your dad, and I want you to know that he isn't your only option. I'd love to have you come work for me at the club with Beck, or you can do whatever the hell you want to do." My dad leaned back in his chair. "You are smart and capable, and you don't need either one of us to make your way in this world, Olly. You are capable of that all on your own."

I glanced over at Olly, but he was staring at my dad. I couldn't get a handle on what he was feeling or what was going through his head. I didn't have a clue until he jerked forward and wrapped his arms around my father's shoulders.

I was shocked by the movement and so was my dad, but he quickly recovered and put his arms around Olly. He patted him on the back before he said something so softly that I couldn't hear. Olly nodded his head against my dad's shoulder before he straightened and took the seat back beside me.

"So, you two are finally doing this, huh?" My mom smiled before running her fingers through the back of my dad's hair.

"Yeah. We are." Olly nodded and reached for my hand. I

let him take it. I would let him take any and everything that
he ever wanted from me.

"Thank God. I never really cared for Ben." She
scrunched up her nose.

"Mom!"

"What?" She looked over at me with a smile. "Don't act
like you didn't already know this. I've been rooting for Olly
all along."

"Thank you." Olly chuckled. "I didn't care for him much
either."

"I'd say not." My dad laughed as he stood. "Olly, let me
know what you decide about work." He reached out for my
mom's hand, and she took it.

"You're also welcome to live in Frankie's room if you don't
want to go back home."

"Umm. That's my room." I laughed because there were
like three different empty guest rooms.

"But you don't live here anymore." She grinned, and I
knew what she was getting at.

"I think Olly would much rather stay in my apartment
with me than stay here, but thank you for the offer." The
only reason that statement could be true was because of me.
Everything about his house was a million times better than
my cramped apartment.

"Thank you." Olly laughed before he looked down at me.
"I have a lot of things to figure out."

"That you do." My dad patted his shoulder as he walked
by us. "But I think you've figured out the most important
part."

CHAPTER 18
FRANKIE

Olly's fingers were still wrapped in mine as we walked into my apartment and closed the door behind us.

I had been living on my own since Dawn moved out over a year ago, and I didn't know why I felt so self-conscious over having Olly here in my space.

He looked around as we walked in, and I dropped my things on the counter and slipped off my shoes.

"So, this is my apartment." I motioned around awkwardly as butterflies took off in my stomach. "I think I'm going to go jump in the shower. Make yourself at home, though."

I walked over to the couch and straightened my old throw blanket. "The remote is right over there."

Olly stepped into my space, and he didn't stop until he wrapped his arms around me. "Where's the bathroom?" he murmured against my forehead.

"Down the hall."

He started heading that way with me still pressed against him, and my feet fumbled underneath me as I had no choice but walk backward in the direction he led me. He stopped outside the bathroom door before grabbing the handle and pushing it open.

"What are you doing?" I chuckled as he pushed us inside. "I know how to shower."

"I know you do, but I don't want to be away from you. Not for a second." He gathered my dress in his hands at my sides before quickly slipping it over my head.

The light from the hallway was creeping into my small bathroom, but I grabbed one of my candles off my shelf and quickly lit it before setting it on the counter. I picked up my toothbrush and shoved it into its holder before tucking my hair behind my ears.

"I'm sorry." I chuckled nervously. "I wasn't expecting you to be coming back here."

"I wasn't planning on being here either." He looked down at me before toeing off his shoes and kicking them to the side. "But I'm not worried about your toothbrush, Frankie."

"I know." I shook my head. "I'm just insanely nervous for some reason."

He walked to the shower and turned on the faucet before I watched him close the stopper on the tub. He ran his hand under the water to check the temperature before turning back to me.

He grabbed my trembling hands between his own and pressed a kiss to my fingertips. "You have nothing to be nervous about. It's just me and you."

"You make me more nervous than anything else in this world."

His gaze darkened as he leaned forward and ran his lips over my shoulder before dropping my bra strap down my arm. "I don't want you to be nervous with me." He pushed my other strap down before reaching behind me and unhooking my bra.

I let it fall down my arms and onto the floor as he watched. He reached behind him and pulled his shirt over his head before he quickly undid his belt and his button. He didn't take his eyes off of me as he dropped his pants to the floor, followed by his underwear.

I stared down at the brace on his knee, and I hated how angry the skin beneath it looked. He reached down to undo the straps, but I quickly dropped to my knees before him.

"Let me help you." I pushed his hands away from his knee before replacing them with my own, and I quickly figured out how to remove the brace while trying my hardest not to hurt him.

"Frankie," he groaned as I placed his brace in the clothes hamper.

"Yeah?" I glanced up at him, and he looked so handsome standing above me as he was.

"You have to get off your fucking knees." He ran a hand through his hair as he stared down at me, and I had never been more mesmerized.

I pressed my fingers into his thighs, and he hissed. "What if I don't want to?"

"As badly as I want this to happen," he swallowed hard, and I looked down at how hard his cock was in front of me, "I want to take a bath and take care of you. I want to fucking talk to you for the first time in what feels like forever."

"Yeah." I nodded, but I couldn't look away. "We do need to talk."

"Frankie, stop looking at me like that and get up." He reached down for me, and I let him help pull me up to my feet.

His gaze roamed over mine before he reached behind him and shut off the water. I dropped my panties down my legs and let him take my hand. He helped me step into the tub, and I groaned as the hot water kissed my legs.

He stepped in behind me, and I watched the small grimace on his face as he straightened out his knee and lowered himself in the tub. He looked up at me expectantly, and I didn't hesitate.

I settled down between his thighs and let my back press against his stomach. His hands lifted some of the water before he slowly let it fall down my chest.

"Relax, Frankie. You're so tense." He wrapped his arm around my chest and tugged me harder against him. He was right, of course. I was tense because I didn't know how to act. I didn't know how to be this with him anymore.

"I'm sorry. I'm just…"

"I know." He murmured against my neck before running his nose along the sensitive skin. "But it's me, Frankie."

I took a deep breath and let my body fall harder against his. I pressed my head into his shoulder and looked up at him.

"I know."

He closed the small gap between us and pressed his lips gently against mine. "Tell me what you want."

"I thought you said…"

"Not like that." He chuckled as his fingers skimmed over my collarbone. "I mean in life. What do you want? What do you dream about?"

I closed my eyes and let the water ease more of the tension from my body as I thought about his question. "Honestly?"

"Yeah." His voice was soft, and his fingers were gentle as they pushed my hair out of my face.

"I don't really know. I feel like I've been just getting by day to day."

"You don't dream of anything?" He lifted my chin until I was forced to look up at him.

"I dream of you."

He was silent for a long moment, and my heart hammered in my chest as I waited for him to say something. Anything.

"You have me, Frankie. For as long as you want me, I'm yours, and even after that." His brown eyes searched mine. "I know you said that loving me scares you, but I promise I will never do anything again that makes you feel that way."

I rolled against him until my chest pressed against his and I could look up at his face. "It scares me because I know that loving you is different, Olly. It scares me because I've been pushing you away for years to protect myself and it hadn't protected me in the least. It's not that I don't trust you. I just don't trust my heart."

"Let your heart do what it wants," he murmured against my mouth before wrapping his arm around my back and tugging me tighter against him. "I promise I'll protect it."

"And then what?" I blinked up at him. "What about school? Are you going to stay in California with Carson?"

"No." He shook his head.

"I think you should."

"Frankie." He sighed, and I could hear the exhaustion in his tone.

"I don't want you to give up anything to be with me. I want you to finish school, and I want you to get back out on the field if that's what you want."

"What I want is to not be without you." He grumbled, and I smiled.

"Then I'll come with you."

He blinked down at me, and I could tell that my words shocked him. "What?"

"If California is where you want to be, then it's where I want to be too."

My body slid against his even harder as he tugged me up to meet his mouth, and he kissed me hard. I was gasping for air by the time he finally let me go.

"I don't want to be in California. I want to come home. I want to live in this apartment with you, if you'll let me. I want to build a future with you right here."

I nodded my head because that was exactly what I wanted too.

"I can enroll in school here and finish my degree. I can work for your dad until we figure things out, but, Frankie, none of that matters. As long as I have you, I'll do whatever it takes to make it work."

"And what if I tell you my dream is to move to Mexico and live in a hut?" I ran my fingers down his chest as I smiled.

"Then we start looking at selling all our shit and getting plane tickets."

I laughed at how serious he was being. "And if my dream is to buy a house with a little white picket fence and have a yard full of babies?"

His hands tightened around me, and he lifted me until I was forced to straddle him. "Then I recommend we go ahead and start trying because the thought of me putting a baby inside of you has me hard as a rock."

I giggled against his mouth, but he wasn't lying. I could

feel how hard he was beneath me. I pushed my wet fingers through his hair, and he looked up at me with a soft smile on his face.

"I love you, Olly." I took a deep breath as I felt the weight of that statement. It was so simple yet so damn complicated, but it was the most honest truth I had.

"And I love you too." He wrapped a hand around my neck and pulled me down into a kiss. "Always."

EPILOGUE
FRANKIE

Three Months Later

The bathroom door opened, and Olly pushed inside as I was trying to reapply my lipstick.

"What are you doing?" I laughed as he stood behind me and pressed against me before meeting my eyes in the mirror.

"I missed you."

He bit down on his bottom lip as his gaze trailed down my body.

"You are insane, Olly. I was just out there." I pointed my hand out into our apartment.

"That's not what I mean and you know it." His hands wrapped around my hips, and he tugged my ass toward him as he stared down to where we met.

I let out a laugh even though I could barely think when he was touching me like that. "This is not happening. Our friends are here."

I wasn't lying. Beck, Josie, Carson, and Allie were all out

in our living room, and there was no way in hell this was happening right now.

"I don't care." He trailed his nose up my neck and his hands tightened against me. "I'm going to tell them all to leave."

I closed my eyes as his tongue caressed the side of my neck before he lightly ran his teeth over the same spot. "No. You are not. That's rude."

"I really don't give a fuck about being rude." His hand snaked around my body, and he pressed his fingers into my dress just over my pussy.

I clung to the bathroom counter as pleasure shot through me. "You don't play fair."

"Not a fan of that either." He looked up at me in the mirror as his hand moved slowly and gently against me. It had the exact opposite effect. I pressed my thighs together as each trail of his fingers made me feel like I was going insane.

"Olly," I whispered his name in warning, but he didn't care.

"I'll make you a deal." He pressed his body harder into mine. "You let me taste your pussy right here, right now, then we can go back out there and finish our night with our friends."

"What's the other option?" I could barely breathe as I watched him in the mirror.

"I go out there and tell them all to get the fuck out so I can fuck you all over this place."

"Oh my God."

He scooped my dress in his hand and his fingers bunched it inch by inch until the only thing between us was my panties. His thumb hooked in the front before he slowly slid them down my hips and let them pool at my feet.

"You're not going to need those either way." He lifted my dress until it was above my hips, and he leaned back slightly to look down at my ass.

"It's up to you, baby."

I opened my mouth to answer him, but I didn't know what he wanted me to say. I felt so insane with lust, but I also didn't want to be rude to our friends. His eyes met mine in the mirror, and he leaned forward to press a kiss on my shoulder.

"I'll give you a minute to decide." He dropped to his knees behind me, and he didn't waste a second before his hands gripped my ass and he spread me apart. His tongue slid through my pussy, and my hips shot forward. He tsked against me before jerking my hips back again.

His mouth was buried against my pussy and his fingers dug into my ass.

"Oh my God, Olly." I covered my mouth with my hand as his tongue flicked over my clit, and I knew that I wouldn't be able to stop him even if I wanted to.

And there wasn't a single ounce of me left that wanted him to.

I pushed my elbows down on the counter as I lifted up onto my tiptoes, and he groaned in approval. "Good fucking girl."

His words hit me as hard as his tongue.

He fucked me with his mouth in a way that I would never get over. He didn't leave a single part of me without his touch. He dove in like he was starving, and my mind couldn't keep up with the way he made me feel.

It was all too strong, too powerful.

"Lift your leg." He grabbed my ankle in his hand and pushed it forward until I had no choice but to bring my knee to the counter where he wanted it. I was so open in front of him, so completely bare, but there wasn't an ounce of timidness left.

He had been destroying that bit by bit every day.

Every bit of insecurity that anyone else had ever created, he demolished it with his touch.

I hadn't realized it at first, but it was now glaringly clear. Olly made me love every inch of myself through the way he loved me.

"Fuck, you're so perfect." He kissed my ass before he went right back to my pussy, and I felt so much more open this way. There wasn't a single chance of me slowing down the orgasm that was already starting to race through my body.

Olly sucked my clit into his mouth, and he built up momentum until I couldn't help but cry out. He didn't stop what he was doing until I pressed my forehead against the counter and tried to muffle my cries with my hands.

My leg slipped but he held me right there, completely open, until he had drawn every bit of my orgasm from my body. Only then did he stand. I tried to catch my breath and didn't look up until I heard his belt clinking behind me.

I looked up to meet his eyes, and he looked so fucking hot behind me.

"I lied to you, baby girl." He unbuttoned his pants and slowly undid the zipper, and I straightened until I was back on my feet in front of him. My legs trembled with the aftereffects of my orgasm.

"About what exactly?" I pushed some hair out of my face as he looked back down my body.

"I'm not going to be able to wait to fuck you." His gaze

met mine in the mirror. "So, you have the choice of the counter or the wall."

"You're giving me a choice?" I grinned. While Olly had become the most supportive guy out of the bedroom when it came to my independence, he tended to be the exact opposite when it came to sex. He took what he wanted, and I had never been turned on more by anyone in my whole life.

"If you want it. But if it's up to me, I'm fucking you against that wall." He nodded to the blank wall behind him. "That way you can watch me fuck you in the mirror. You can see every fucking thing I do to you."

I swallowed hard.

"Is that what you want?"

"Yes." I nodded just before he spun me around to face him.

He gripped my jaw in his hand as he looked over my face. He was so damn handsome, and he only became more so when he looked at me like he was now. He looked at me like he was as in love with me as I was him, and I never wanted him to stop.

"Kiss me, Frankie."

I did. I leaned forward and pressed my lips to his, and he kissed me exactly like he had my pussy. Thoroughly and intensely. I could taste myself on his lips, and I pressed my thighs together as the memories of what he had just done to my body hit me.

Olly dropped his hands and pressed his fingers into the back of my knees. He lifted me, and I had no choice but to cling onto his shoulders and hold on as he spun us and pressed my back into the wall.

"They're going to start wondering where we are," I muttered against his mouth.

"I don't give a fuck what they think." His fingers dug into my ass as he lifted me higher and pressed his hips into me. He quickly pushed his pants off, and they fell to the floor around his ankles. "Nothing is going to stop me from fucking you right now. No one except you."

I shook my head because we both knew that it wasn't going to be me. I wanted him as badly as he wanted me.

"Then watch me." He leaned back and pulled his cock free between us. He pressed the head of it against my opening and used his fingers to spread my wetness along the length of him before he glanced back up at me. "God, you are so gorgeous."

"Fuck me, Olly." I tightened my legs around his back and pulled him closer to me.

He slid inside, and I moaned as he filled me up. I felt so damn full, and it was the most delicious pleasure. "My pleasure."

He wrapped one arm around my back to hold me against him before pressing the other against the wall above my head, then he fucked me.

He slammed into me hard before he slowly pulled back, and his mouth met mine again. He kissed me with as much vigor as his hips used against mine, and I clung to his shoulders.

"Goddamn, I love you." He slid in and out of me, and I let my head fall back against the wall.

"I love you too."

His hand tangled in my hair at the base of my skull, and he pulled hard until I was forced to look back up. "Watch us in the mirror, Frankie. Look how fucking beautiful you are while I fuck you."

I tightened my hold on him as I did what he said. I had a

perfect view of both of us, of his perfect ass, and it felt so erotic.

His tongue ran over my neck before he clamped down with his teeth, and my hips surged forward.

"Look how perfect we fit together," he whispered against my skin, and my legs tightened as another orgasm built and built inside of me.

Olly leaned back so he could look down at where we were connected, and he fucked me harder. He ran a hand down my body before he pressed his thumb against my clit, and he looked so possessive as he watched us.

"You are mine, Frankie."

"I'm yours," I answered immediately because there wasn't a single doubt in my mind.

"Always." He lifted his hand before slapping it down against my pussy, and my orgasm surged through me.

My pussy clamped down around him as he slammed into me over and over, and I knew by the way his back tensed that he was right there with me.

"Say it, Frankie," he groaned against me.

"I'll always be yours, Olly. Always." He pressed his face into my neck as he came hard with a loud groan, and I pushed my fingers through his hair as I tried to pull him closer.

We stayed just like that for a long moment before he pushed off the wall with me still in his arms and turned to put me on the counter. He left me there as he grabbed a washcloth and ran it under the water.

I spread my legs as he moved back in front of me and gently pressed the warm cloth against my pussy and cleaned me up. I winced as he ran it over the most sensitive parts of me, and I knew that I hadn't had enough of Olly tonight. I was going to be thinking about him until everyone else left.

Oh my God. Everyone else.

"Olly, shit." I pushed against his shoulders and jumped down off the counter.

"What?" He pressed against me and refused to let me move.

"Everyone is still here."

"I'm aware, baby."

"And I just let you fuck me," I hissed.

"I'm more than aware of that fact too." He pushed some of my hair behind my ear.

"We need to go back out there."

"Not until you kiss me." He ran his nose along my jaw.

"Olly!"

"Frankie." He chuckled. "You're not leaving this room until you give me your fucking lips."

I knew that he was being serious, so I did just that. I kissed him until I no longer cared that anyone was waiting for us, and only then did he pull away.

He looked at me one last time before he opened the door and stepped outside. "Sorry, guys. Frankie needed my help in there."

I was going to kill him.

CHAPTER 1

I turned the page and gripped the paperback harder in my hands. It didn't matter how many times those ruffled pages had been turned by my fingers, my heart still thumped against my chest.

I ate the words up one by one, relishing in the story, anxious to get to the part I knew was coming. The page slipped through my fingers as I turned it quickly, not missing a beat as I saw the winged warrior so clearly in my mind. He lifted his sword, ready to fight for his mate, and the loud buzzing rang through the room making me jump.

My paperback clutched to my chest, I looked around the room at all the people busying themselves with their laundry. My dryer still spun beside me, and I cringed I saw a pair of my lace panties slam against the dryer door and gyrate around like they were putting on a show.

The laundromat was packed today, but I had completely forgotten where I was. The smell of laundry detergent filled my nose and blocked the scent of citrus that clung to the skin of the warrior I had so unmistakably smelled a moment before.

A young boy, probably no more than three years old, ran in a circle around my chair. His toy beat against every surface he could find as he smiled wildly. His mother, on the other hand, looked like she was at her wit's end. She chased behind him, balancing laundry in one hand while stretching the other out to grab him. He grinned up at me as he headed my way again, and I imagined him as the mighty warrior in my story. Impossible to tame.

I waved at him as he ran by me, and he came to a sudden stop. He stared up at me, curiosity filling his innocent face, and pointed to the book in my hand.

"Whad are you doing?" His t's sounded like a d, and I smiled at how adorable he was.

"I'm reading." I looked up at his mom who stopped in a huff behind him. "What are you doing?"

"Running from monsters." He grinned before looking over his shoulder at his mom.

"Really?" My voice was in awe. "That's what I'm reading about right now."

He cocked his head and looked down at my book. "You like monsters?"

I shook my head. "No, but I love to read about the warriors who fight them."

His eyes lit up, and he inched closer to me.

"If you want, you can sit beside me, and I'll read to you while your mom finishes her laundry." I glanced at the mom for her permission, but the sudden relief in her eyes was all I needed. She tucked a piece of loose hair behind her ear as her son crawled up in the chair beside me.

"Thank you," she silently mouthed the words to me as she set her laundry basket on the table across from us.

I smiled at her as I opened the book to page one.

The little boy sat attentively as I read the words to him. His eyes got big as saucers as I described the monsters in the book, and he wrinkled his nose when I talked about the girl with golden hair.

We had just finished the first chapter when his mom squats down in front of him.

"Are you ready to go, Jonah?" Her hands reached out and tied his shoelace that had started to come undone.

"We're reading, Mama." He grinned up at me and I returned it.

"I know." She smiled at me as well. "But it's time to go to the park."

"Yay." He pumped his tiny fist in the air and quickly jumped from his seat.

The boy who sat attentively while I read to him was long gone, and he was once again running around full of energy.

"Thank you so much." His mother's eyes tracked his every movement. "You don't know how much I appreciate that."

"It's no big deal." I looked away from her and tucked my paperback into my bag.

"It is." She held my gaze, and I squirmed in my seat. "Just thank you."

"You're welcome."

I went to my dryer as they headed out the door and pulled out my already cold laundry. I should have folded our clothes right then and there, but they were already cold which meant the wrinkles were already setting in. My roommate, Brooke, would be mad, but I was dying to get home to finish the rest of my book.

With my basket against my hip, I awkwardly smiled at the man who sat closest to me before I grabbed my bag and headed out the door. If my roommate and I were responsible adults, we would have gotten our dryer fixed weeks ago. But adulting was hard and buying makeup always seemed more important to Brooke while blowing my paycheck on books would always be more important to me.

The laundromat was a short walk from our apartment building. I stared at the elevator as I stepped through the heavy glass door. It had been broken for the last four days, and I had never hated living on the fifth floor more.

I hiked my laundry basket higher on my hip, and I pulled the door open to the stairwell as I began my long journey home. Each flight had ten stairs in it, and I counted each step as if I was reaching the end of a marathon. Surely someone would be at the top with a congratulatory cookie or something. What I wouldn't give to be living in the book I was currently reading. Then the hero could just lift me in his arms and fly me to the fifth floor.

I snorted out loud at how big of a nerd I was and completely missed the body that came barreling down the stairway toward me. I jumped out of the way with only seconds to spare and several pieces of my freshly laundered clothes fell onto the stairs. They looked like they probably hadn't been cleaned in quite some time, and I quickly squatted down and began grabbing my clothes off the ground. It was as if there was a five-second rule for the amount of time that could lapse before they caught herpes.

I hadn't even looked up at the person who almost caused the near death collision. There was no time to spare. My clothes were collecting bacteria with every second that ticked by, and there was no way I was going back to the laundromat before next week.

"I'm so sorry," a deep southern accent pulled my attention away from my "Don't trust the muggles" shirt that my hand was currently hovering over.

"No worries," I started to say, but I wasn't sure what actually came out of my mouth because when I looked up, I almost fell on my ass.

He was picking up clothes, my clothes, and throwing them in my basket. While I, like a total creeper, stared at him in awe. His jaw was square and had just a touch of scruff covering it. His hair was light brown and styled perfectly in that "I just woke up, ran my hands through my hair, and managed to look like a supermodel" kind of way. My hand was twitching to run my fingers through it to see if it was as soft as it looked. He had on a white T-shirt that stretched across his fit chest and a pair of black running shorts that showed off his muscular calves.

I ran my gaze up his body but stopped dead when I realized there was something dangling from his strong callused fingers. I would have given anything to see my red lacy panties that I was so ashamed of moments before staring back at me. Instead of one of the only sexy panties I owned, the piece of fabric that he held up in front of him with a quizzical look on his face was none other than my loyal, trusty, always hold us together Spanx.

Kill. Me. Now.

"What are these?"

My eyes darted up from the offensive piece of fabric that had the power to suck in my stomach when my will power had all but given up and stared into his laughing, chocolate brown eyes. I reached out and ripped my Spanx from his hand and buried them deep in the basket. I spotted my red lacy panties that probably matched my face at that moment and mentally cussed them for not stepping up when I was in need.

A deep chuckle echoed against the walls in the stairwell and it felt like there were thirty people in there laughing at me.

"Umm..." I trailed off because I didn't know what to say to him. I sure as hell wasn't about to tell him that he was just holding my Spanx.

His phone rang as soon as I opened my mouth to speak again and saved me from making a bigger fool of myself, and he smiled at me and shook his phone in my direction.

"Well, it looks like we'll have to save this conversation for another time."

Over my dead body.

I didn't say that out loud though. I just thought it as I watched his ass jog down the stairs and away from me. I waited patiently for something to jiggle as his feet pounded against each step, but his muscles bunching and releasing didn't count. As he rounded the corner to go down the next set of stairs, he looked back up at me smirking, and I realized I was just standing there with my basket full of shame staring at him.

I quickly spun around holding my hand over my clothes being careful not to drop anything again and headed up my last flight of stairs. I guess it's true what they say about the likelihood of you having a wreck is greater when you're within five minutes from your home because I only had about six stairs before I would have been in the clear.

Instead, I managed to embarrass myself in front one of the hottest men I had ever met.

I busted through my apartment door and Brooke looked up at me from painting her pink toenails like I was crazy.

"Bad week at the laundromat?" she asked before she blew on her freshly painted toes.

"You could say that." I set down the basket on the coffee table and plopped down on the couch across from her.

"What happened?"

"Well to start, the laundromat was packed and it took me a good ten minutes to find an open washer, but then I get home and things only got worse."

"Why?" She finally looked up from her pedicure and gave me her full attention.

"I was walking up the stairs lost in my own world when some guy came crashing into me and knocking our clean clothes all over the floor." My story was very dramatic, and I waved my hands in the air to show all the different directions our clothes landed.

Brooke leaned closer toward me. "Was he hot?"

I wasn't at all surprised by her response.

"I'm not even sure how that is even relevant, but yes, he was incredibly hot."

"What did he look like?" she interrupted me.

"Really, Brooke? I'm trying to tell a story here." I acted exasperated even though I wasn't.

"Sorry. Please continue." She waved her hand like she was the queen finally giving me permission to talk.

"Like I said, he ran straight into me and our clothes were everywhere. He helped me pick them up."

"What a gentleman."

I gave her the evil eye, and she pretended to zip her lips and throw the key over her shoulder.

"When I picked up the last shirt, I looked up at him, and he had my Spanx, my Spanx," I pointed at my chest, "dangling from his fingers."

Brooke's mouth was hanging open at that point, and I was highly surprised that nothing was coming out.

"He asked me what they were." By the sound of my voice, you would have thought he had asked me for a quickie on the stairs.

"What did you say?" Brooke squeaked.

"I did what any sane woman would do. I snatched them out of his hand and didn't reply. His phone rang right after that and saved me from having to talk about it any further."

"Oh my God." Brooke laughed.

"Exactly. I just hope that he doesn't actually live in this building. Maybe he was leaving a one-night stand."

Brooke laughed again and resumed painting her toes.

"What?" I asked.

"I hope you're right because two super-hot guys just moved in next door to us," she pointed to the wall to our left indicating the apartment that we shared a wall with, "and I invited them both for dinner tomorrow night."

CHAPTER 2

Falling asleep that night was horrible. I tossed and turned and thought about how big of a fool I made of myself in front of my possible new neighbor. I was still praying that he was running out after a one-night stand, but knowing my luck, that wasn't likely. He would probably be sitting across from me at dinner tomorrow night while I did my best to avoid looking at him.

I pulled out my Kindle and relied on my latest book boyfriend to help me get out of my own head and fall asleep. It was a really bad plan because once I got started, I didn't want to put it down. It was around one in the morning when I finally turned it off, and I had to be up early in the morning to meet my client for a shoot.

The sound of my alarm blaring woke me up and I slammed my hand against my phone to shut it up. I felt like I had only been asleep for about ten minutes, and I had every intention to take advantage of the snooze feature. My alarm continued to blare, and after pressing every button on the phone I could find, I finally peeked one of my eyes open to see what the heck was wrong with the torture device.

The light from my phone almost blinded me in my pitch-black room causing me to close my eyes again until I realized that I had just seen two twenty-five on the screen. I sat up in bed and looked around my room. The music was still blaring, and it took me a minute before I realized it was "Take Your Time" by Sam Hunt. While it was a song I loved, it wasn't something I wanted waking me up in the middle of the night unless Sam himself was there to serenade me.

The lyrics were muffled but the beat of the song was clear, vibrating against the wall behind my head. I turned toward the wall and squinted my eyes as if they had enough hate power to get the music to shut off without me having to climb out of bed.

The floor was cold as I walked like a zombie into Brooke's room. I could barely see her through the hall light that was shining into her room, but I knew she was sprawled out in the middle of her queen size bed taking up all of the room. When we first moved in together, we had to share a bed until we could afford another one. It was the hardest few months of my life. I had never been cuddled so hard. We had fallen in love with the apartment, and we decided having the apartment was worth not having everything else in the beginning. I didn't realize at that time that Brooke was a complete bed hog and would attempt to smother me to death in my sleep with her cuddles. In the year that we had lived here, we worked hard to furnish it in a style that was both Brooke's and mine. So, it was half girly and half nerdy.

"Shit," I whisper yelled when I felt something stab my foot.

I hopped on one foot and looked down at the eyelash

curler that caused my foot to feel like it needed to be amputated. I had always thought that thing looked like it was used to cause suffering in its victims. Not beauty.

I limped my way to Brooke's bed and plopped down beside her causing her to bounce on the mattress. She didn't even notice. The music was still blaring through the apartment, but it was much quieter on this side of the hall.

"Brooke." I shook her shoulder and her blonde hair swayed with the movement.

"Hello." I shook harder. "Earth to Brooke."

There was no movement whatsoever other than what I was causing. She was completely dead to the world. When I bounced up and down on the mattress and tickled her foot with no results, I chalked her up as a lost cause.

I momentarily considered just forgetting about the music and trying to go back to bed, but when I walked back out into the hall the song changed and cheering broke out.

"Are you kidding me?" I said out loud to myself.

The sound of several voices drunkenly singing the lyrics to a song I didn't recognize had me marching my way out of my apartment and to the apartment next door.

I knocked on the door and waited several moments with no answer. The singing was still going strong, and I wasn't surprised that they didn't hear me. I raised my fist in the air and pounded again, this time louder.

The door swung open and the voices that I thought were loud a moment ago seemed to triple in volume. A tall man who could only be described as a dark Adonis stood in the doorway. His hair was a dark brown that complemented his dark tan perfectly. I couldn't tell what color his eyes were because I was completely distracted by the smooth smile that took over his handsome face.

"Hello, gorgeous. I'm Liam."

He stuck out his large hand and slipped my much smaller, slightly sweaty one in his.

"Are you here for the party?" His gaze roamed down my body and stopped on my chest. I followed his path and tensed when I realized I was still in my Harry Potter pajama shorts that left nothing to the imagination and a white tank top with no bra that literally directed you on which way your imagination should go.

I tucked a strand of my raven black hair behind my ear and crossed my arms.

"No. I'm Kennedy. I live next door." I shuffled on my feet because I hated confrontation. "I was actually coming to ask you to turn the music down."

"Yo, Liam. What's going on?" The deep southern drawl caused me to pull my gaze away from the smile on Liam's face to see none other than the guy from the stairs.

"Well Tucker, our little neighbor here is asking for us to turn down the noise." Liam pointed to me and instantly got a strike against him for referring to me as little. I wasn't a little girl, and I hated being referred to as such just because I was a woman.

"Hello again." He leaned against the doorframe and I watched as his eyes turned to me.

"You've met?" Liam asked as he turned to look at me.

"Yeah. She's the girl I was telling you about earlier."

"So anyway," I interrupted. "I'd love to stay and chat, but some of us have to be up early for work so if you could turn the music down just a bit, I'd appreciate it."

I turned away from them without waiting for a response. I could feel them watching me as I walked and tugged at the hem of my shorts to cover myself.

"Wait," Tucker called out, halting me, and I slowly turned to him. "What's your name?"

I blinked at his question and tucked a loose strand of hair behind my ear.

"Why?"

"Why do I want to know your name?" he asked.

I nodded my head.

"We're neighbors now. I think we should at least know each other's names."

"Well, Tucker." I took a step back toward my door. "As one good neighbor to another," I cocked an eyebrow at him. "Turn down the music and I'll think about telling you my name."

Then I scurried to my door and slammed it shut behind me.

CHAPTER 3

I felt like I had a hangover, and I wasn't even at a party last night. Instead, the party came to me, at least through my wall. The music did get turned down after I went next door, and I couldn't be certain, but I think that most of their party guests left shortly after as well. I had buried my head under my pillow to block out the embarrassment that I felt after my interaction with Tucker and Liam.

Liam was hot, really hot. He had dark brown hair and a tan to match it. As soon as I laid eyes on him, I knew exactly why Brooke had invited them over for dinner.

But he had nothing on Tucker.

When Liam had opened the door, I had breathed a sigh of relief that it wasn't Tucker. After our incident on the stairs, I wasn't sure if I could face him.

I should have known that I wasn't that lucky.

As soon as he made his way to the door, I instantly felt myself become more awkward. More nervous.

And I knew he could tell.

I think I managed to get about four hours of sleep total. I

was sleep-deprived, grumpy, and in desperate need of coffee. Slinging my purse over my shoulder, I grabbed all of my camera equipment and made my way out of the apartment. I glanced at Tucker's quiet door as I passed by.

When I arrived downtown, the couple whose engagement photos I was taking was waiting for me next to an older industrial building. It was kind of my thing. I loved photography. Every single thing about it. I loved taking something that may have looked normal or unimpressive to someone else and showing it to the world through a new perspective. But my true passion was capturing architecture.

I absolutely loved it.

There was something about the sharp lines of an old or new building. The way it stood strong, breaking through the sky in an almost impossible way. The unique curves and details that are so easily looked over. There was something about a structure that was once so grand being forgotten. The delicate rust, the years of wear from the hands that once worked there. I could capture it with my lens and give it life again.

I started photographing weddings, engagements, children, etc... for the money. While it wasn't my true passion, I did love doing it, and it paid the bills. There were a lot more people in the market for wedding photos than there were for architecture. But when I did get a chance to do them, I jumped at the opportunity.

The building that the newly engaged couple was standing by was covered in bright red paint that had chipped and worn off through the years. The brown brick peeked through the bright color and gave the building character that I was sure it lacked when it was freshly painted. It was my favorite building to shoot engagement photos next to.

The couple looked to be almost the exact opposite of each other. She was small and delicate somehow with her straight brown hair and bright smile. Her fiancé, on the other hand, sported a massive beard and a man bun on the top of his head. He towered over her, but somehow, they fit together so perfectly.

"Hey, guys." I waved at the couple, Mia and Rob. "It's nice to finally meet you."

Mia walked straight up to me and pulled me into a hug. It wasn't really my thing, but her smile and good spirit were pretty infectious.

"Hi, Kennedy. We are so happy to meet you. We are so excited for today."

I chuckled as I pulled myself out of her grip and stuck my hand out to Rob.

"Hi. I'm Rob."

"Hey, Rob. Killer man bun." I pointed to the top of his head.

"Thanks." His sweet smile took over his face, and I instantly knew that I was going to like the both of them.

I could usually tell within minutes of meeting the people I was going to photograph if we were going to mesh well or not, and it was important. The people who I felt somehow connected to always ended up with stellar photos. I liked to think that all my photos were good, but there was just something extra special about those. Something magical.

"So," I started pulling my camera out of my bag, "do the two of you have any specific ideas in mind?"

"Honestly," Mia looked over at Rob, "we instantly fell in love with your work as soon as we saw it. We really trust you and what you think will look best."

"Thank you. You two will make some amazing photos." I smiled at her, but on the inside, I was beaming.

It wasn't uncommon for me to get complimented on my work, but every time someone did, it filled me with so much pride that I thought I would burst at the seams. I don't know if it was something I would ever get used to, but I hoped that I didn't.

"Okay. I'd like to start at the front of the building if that's okay with you all. It is the best place to catch the sunlight."

"That sounds great." Mia beamed at me, and I couldn't help being as excited for the shoot as she was.

We went through several poses and moved through downtown taking advantage of all the older buildings as a backdrop. Mia and Rob's love was easy to capture, and their laughter throughout the entire shoot made my job not only easy but fun. By the time we were done, I had a camera full of amazing photos begging for me to edit and a large smile on my face. I hugged the couple goodbye and told them that I couldn't wait to shoot their wedding which was one hundred percent true. Weddings weren't my favorite thing in the world, but when it was for a couple like them, I couldn't wait.

By the time I made it back to our apartment, I was tired but blissfully happy. There was just something about holding my camera in my hand and using the click of my finger to capture something that had nothing to do with me that seemed to make my worries go out the window. It had a way of centering me that I hadn't been able to find with anything else.

I walked through our front door and the smell of marinara sauce hit my nose. It smelled delicious, but it was such a rare thing for Brooke to cook that I was a little concerned about what she was making. But then the sound of male laughter hit my ears and panic filled my chest when I remembered that she had invited our new neighbors over for dinner.

Screw her and her neighborliness.

I tiptoed through the living room to make it to my room before they heard me, but Brooke had some sort of spidey sense and knew I was there without ever seeing me.

"Kennedy, is that you?" she called through the apartment.

"Yeah. I'm just putting my bags down," I yelled back then dragged my butt to my bedroom to give myself a pep talk to come back out and face Tucker.

I took my time and went ahead and plugged my camera into my computer so my images from today would download. I stood in front of the mirror and looked at myself in my black leggings, white blouse, and black flats and decided that nothing else I put on would really make me look any better. I ran a brush through my hair even though it was still stick straight from this morning, then I finally made my way out of my room and headed toward the kitchen.

Tucker was in the living room bent down looking at my book collection with a beer in his hand when I walked in. It took everything inside me not to pull him away from my babies, but I decided that confrontation with our new neighbor for the second time in less than twenty-four hours probably wasn't a good idea.

"Who's got such an eclectic taste in reading materials?" Tucker asked without realizing I was standing behind him.

"That would be me." I walked up beside him when he looked over his shoulder with a large smirk on his face. "Brooke isn't much of a reader."

"I didn't take you for a romance fan." He took a sip of his beer while looking up and down my body making every inch of my skin tingle.

"What exactly did you take me for then?" I put my hands on my hips. I didn't know what it was about him, but almost every word that came out of his mouth seemed to put me on the defense.

"I don't know. Maybe something less fun or romantic. Zombies maybe?" His grin was even bigger now, and I knew he was trying to get a rise out of me.

"I'm not that into zombies actually. I'm more into fantasy." I shrugged my shoulders.

"Uh huh. So Harry Potter and," he ran his fingers across my favorite books, "A Court of Thorn and Roses. You're one of those girls then." He said it as if he knew everything he would ever need to know about me before taking another sip of his beer, and I fought the urge to pull the bottle away from his lips and smash it over his head.

"Let me guess," I said dramatically. "You're probably really into football, and I bet you're killing it in your fantasy league. But your true champion status probably comes from beer pong."

He laughed deep and long, and I could feel a small smile tugging on my lips even though I didn't want it to be there.

"You're a firecracker, aren't you?" He cocked his head to the side and looked me over again as if he was trying to figure me out.

I was about to come back with some awesome rebuttal that I hadn't even thought of yet when he pointed over my shoulder at the photos on the wall.

"Where did you get these pictures from?" He walked

toward one of my shots of an old abandoned barn I had taken a couple years ago. "They are amazing."

"They are just something I collect." I looked away from him before he could read the lie on my face. I wasn't sure why I lied to him. Actually, that's a lie too. I knew exactly why I didn't tell him that I took them. I didn't want him to make a joke out of my work. He was so easygoing. Full of jokes and conniving smirks. My photography was sacred to me, and I couldn't handle him saying something bad about it.

"Dinner's ready," Brooke called out to us.

Tucker waved his hand toward the kitchen and waited for me to walk in front of him. I thought I heard him chuckle when I walked past, but when I looked back at him, he had his beer up against his smiling lips.

Liam was already sitting at our dining room table while Brooke weaved her way around the space and set the last of dinner on the table. I quickly sat down beside Liam in hopes that I wouldn't have to sit next to Tucker. It was childish, I knew that but I hadn't even known him two full days yet, and he was driving me crazy.

I didn't know what made me think my plan would actually work. Tucker pulled out the seat next to me and plopped down with that same irritating smirk on his lips. He knew that I was trying to avoid sitting next to him, I could read it on his face, but I could also tell that getting on my nerves was becoming a game to him.

I wasn't sure what had caused my irritation with him, but I did know that it was overwhelming. He was hot as hell, and he knew it. There was no way that he didn't. He reminded me of every douche bag I had ever dated.

You know the type.

In the beginning, he would treat me as if I was perfect. He would open the door, take me out, and be the guy of my dreams, but as time would roll on, my flaws would come out.

"You're so beautiful for a bigger girl." I couldn't tell you how many times I had heard that non-compliment. It baffled me how anyone ever thought they were giving me kudos for managing to be pretty and thick. My second favorite was, "If you lost a few pounds, you'd be so much prettier."

I always wanted to respond with a, "Yeah? You'd be so much hotter with a few extras inches on your dick," but I never did. I just smiled and pretended like calling me pretty with a disclaimer should make me happy.

I was a confident girl. My photography was amazing, I could beat just about anyone I knew in trivia, and I was pretty, but the one thing that always seemed to bring my confidence down a notch was my weight.

I had struggled with my weight for years. I wasn't obese, but I had enough cushion for me to be in a different category when describing women. My good luck with men was directly related to my insecurities. I was always attracted to the guy who made me feel good about myself in the beginning then dug into my spirit little by little as time went on. I always knew it was happening, and I always said I wouldn't allow it to happen again, until it did.

My last boyfriend, Sam, was the prime example. I thought he was perfect. I wanted him to be perfect, but the only thing he was good at was being a lousy boyfriend. He blatantly told me that he thought I needed to lose weight, and after I cried my eyes out to Brooke, I marched my too big for him ass over to his apartment to break it off. I was pumped. My feminist flag was flying high, and I wasn't going to let anyone make me feel bad about myself. Especially not him. Only it wasn't that simple. I walked in on him sleeping with a stick thin girl who I had seen hanging around his group of friends.

Her name was Ashley, and she was always looking for a man to sink her teeth into. Specifically, a man with money. I had once heard her talking to her friend in the bathroom about how she needed to "lock down" one of Sam's friends who had enough money to take care of her for life. She didn't know that I was in the stall, and I didn't know she was such a whore. But she knew I was dating him.

Sam didn't act remorseful at all when I caught him, and neither did she. She just smiled a smile at me that made me want to smack it off her perfect face, but instead, I walked out and didn't look back. I promised myself I would never date a guy like him again. I hardened my heart to the bullshit, and I worked out my aggression at the gym. I managed to lose about thirty pounds since he taught me that valuable life lesson, but I didn't attribute my weight loss to the heartbreak. All that credit went to me and me alone. It was something I wanted, so I did it.

But I still wasn't comfortable with my weight loss. I got more attention from guys when we went out, and when I looked in the mirror, I loved what I saw. I would never be a thin girl, but I was learning to love my curves. I did still have a habit of pulling down my top when it wasn't perfectly in place. It annoyed the crap out of Brooke.

She saw me as a bombshell, but as my best friend, her opinion was jaded. I knew I would grow more comfortable in my new body, but it would take time. I was still a big girl. I just had a lot more tone than I used to.

I think that was what annoyed me the most about Tucker. The first time I met him, he held one of my most uncomfortable, both literally and figuratively, items of clothing in his hand. While I didn't have the same stomach that I once did, I still wore my Spanx from time to time to make me feel more comfortable, and I didn't need Tucker to be privy to my insecurities.

I didn't even know the guy, but I didn't trust him as far as I could throw him. He was too good looking. His smile was too slick, and his dimples were too deep. Yes. I know how ridiculous I sound, but everything about him was getting on my nerves.

"Where are the two of you from?" Brooke passed the food around to Liam and Tucker, and I thanked God she was there. Otherwise, this dinner would be completely awkward.

"A really small town in Tennessee. You've probably never heard of it." Liam chuckled.

"What brought you all here?" I grabbed a breadstick out of the basket that Liam just handed me.

"Business ventures," Tucker said while looking over at Liam.

"That's vague." I snorted. "Does that mean you're selling drugs or something?"

"No." Liam laughed. "That would probably be more lucrative though. We're actually working on a restaurant downtown."

"So, Brooke." Tucker's voice pulled me out of my own head, and I realized I was wadding up my napkin in my lap. "Are you a professional cook?"

I snorted and every set of eyes turned to me including Brooke's narrowed ones.

"Sorry. There was something in my throat." I avoided looking at Brooke because I knew I would be getting a death glare. The reason why? She was a horrible cook. One of the worst. But she had about three meals in her arsenal that she was damn good at. Steer outside of those three meals, and you would probably be puking for a week. Luckily, tonight she had cooked her top recipe. Lasagna.

"Well, it tastes amazing," Liam said to Brooke and shot her a smile that was causing her to practically swoon before my eyes.

I bit into my own food before I could manage to make any more embarrassing noises, but I groaned when the flavor hit my tongue. How someone could cook something so good then butcher everything else was beyond me.

"Is it as good as it sounds?" Tucker's voice was low but full of humor.

I swallowed the food that was still in my mouth. "What?"

"You were practically moaning over there. I think I know what you sound like when you're about to come." He chuckled at his own joke.

"If that is what it sounds like when you're about to make a woman come then you seriously need some practice."

Liam choked on a sip of his drink and then a coughing fit started that was mixed with laughter. Tucker was laughing too. My insult didn't faze him.

"Like I said, firecracker." He took another sip of beer, and I was suddenly jealous of the bottle that was touching his lips.

"Like I said, practice." I winked at him before cracking my own smile, and internally I shivered a little because I didn't think he would need any practice at all.

CHAPTER 4

Thump.

Thump, thump.

Thump.

Peeking one eye open, I stared around my pitch-black bedroom.

Thump.

I looked over my head and stared at the wall behind me. I felt like I was having deja vu except this time it was pounding on the wall instead of loud music.

Thump, thump.

My head rattled with the loud hammering behind me, and I could have sworn that I could almost feel vibrations in my bed.

I set up and stared at the wall. Mad wasn't a good enough description of what I was. I needed sleep, and I wanted it uninterrupted.

I wasn't sure which of my new neighbors shared a wall with me, but I knew that I was ready to kill him. They had literally just left our apartment a few hours before. *Did they have a speed dial of tramps just waiting for their call?*

Thump.

I guess that was my answer.

Those man whores.

It ran through my mind that I should have just got up and went to sleep on the couch, but it was my house, damn it. I wanted to sleep in my own bed. In peace.

Light flooded the room when I clicked on my lamp, and I went searching for my headphones and iPod. I pressed the power button and smiled at the image of a cat wearing sunglasses pointing its paw at me saying "You're Purrfect."

I entered my passcode and scrolled through my music to find something that I could manage to sleep through.

Thump, thump, thump.

It would definitely need a beat.

My hand hesitated over the song choices and with a simple title of a song, I got a new idea. I quickly grabbed my speakers and set them on my nightstand, but instead of pointing them where I could hear them, I faced them directly against the wall. I clicked on the song before turning my volume to full blast. I knew it wouldn't bother Brooke. The speakers could be next to her ear, and it wouldn't wake her up.

The lyrics to "Scrub" by TLC blared through the speakers, and I flew back on my bed in a fit of giggles. I could no longer hear the pounding against my wall, but I wasn't sure if it was because they had stopped or because my music was too loud.

Then it happened.

There was a series of rapid knocks against my wall. I paused my music and waited to see what would happen next as my heart raced in my chest. I stared at the wall as if I was expecting someone to jump through it at any moment.

My heart beat louder than the thumping moments before.

A deep laughter echoed through the wall then I heard his gruff voice yell, "Well played, Firecracker."

...

The next day I didn't have a shoot scheduled, and I was thankful that I didn't have to wake up early for work because I had an appointment, *yes, appointment,* scheduled with my mother. Sleep was desperately needed for an appointment with my mother, and I couldn't miss it either. If you missed an appointment with my mother, you would never hear the end of it.

You're so irresponsible.

Maybe if you had a real career, you would understand the importance of keeping appointments.

That one was my favorite.

Neither of my parents approved of my "little hobby" as they so nicely put it. They had expected me to become a doctor like my brother or possibly a lawyer like my dad. I think my mother's biggest dream was for me to marry a doctor or a lawyer like she did, but I disappointed them both and followed my dream. They refused to acknowledge my photography as an actual career.

It didn't matter how much money I made or how many times I got recognized, it would always be a hobby to them. It didn't matter that I was booked out for a few months.

I liked to lie to myself and say that their opinion didn't matter, but deep down, it mattered way too much. But every time someone raved about my work, it seemed to chip away a small amount of the weight of their disapproval. I always avoided them long enough that I almost felt weightless by the time I saw them again, but they never failed to lay it on me again.

We were meeting at a trendy restaurant downtown close to my favorite buildings. I would have settled for a burger joint, but my mom didn't do greasy food or hole in the wall restaurants. She couldn't have it affecting her body or her image. She would drop dead before one of her "friends" saw her in a place like that.

I walked into the restaurant, but I didn't have to approach the hostess because I could see my mother sitting in the middle of the restaurant where she could see everyone and everyone could clearly see her. She smiled up at me but I could see the fakeness in her cheery expression as I always had. She looked down my body, and I almost saw her physically jolt back when she saw the jeans that covered my legs.

Her overly sweet perfume hit my nose as soon as I plopped down in the seat across from her. It was a familiar smell and one that always made my stomach turn.

"Could you not dress appropriately just once?" She acted exasperated but her voice was low so no one around us could hear that she was anything but perfectly happy.

I looked across the table at her flawlessly pressed pink button-down top that I was sure was either tucked into trousers or a pencil skirt. There wasn't much variety where that was concerned. Her perfect brown hair was pulled back in a tight bun that made her face look even more severe than the Botox injections alone could provide. As if she needed the help.

"It's nice to see you too." I pulled my napkin off the table in front of me and laid it in my lap.

The waiter arrived at the table before she could get out another snarky comment, and I ordered a Coke while she ordered a mimosa.

"Drinking at lunch. You must have had a hard day."

"Don't sass your mother in public." She straightened her already perfectly straight top while smiling at the table next to us.

"So what did you want the appointment for?" I cut to the chase.

She looked me over again, and I could feel her judgment with every inch of skin her eyes passed over. I could feel it as if it was a living breathing thing.

"Why don't you let me make you an appointment at my salon so they can do something with your hair? You're not a teenager anymore."

I fingered a strand on my straight hair then looked back up at hers. I didn't know what she expected of me. Why I had to fit some perfect mold.

Her stern eyes were boring into mine when I didn't answer her. "Did you see the new restaurant that they are putting in down the block? They should have just torn down that building and started over."

"I'm not really into new buildings. I like things that are old and decrepit. What's it called?"

She rolled her eyes. "Rock Bottom. How tacky."

Before I could tell her that I really liked it, the waiter returned to our table and set our drinks in front of us.

"Are you ready to order?"

"Yes." She didn't ask me if I was ready. "I would like a house salad with the vinaigrette dressing on the side. Do you know if the dressing is made fresh?" She didn't give him a chance to answer. "If not, I would like it freshly made."

"Yes, ma'am." He turned to me.

"I'll take the cheeseburger with fries, please."

He smiled at me kindly then took our menus and walked away to probably spit in our food.

"Should you really be eating a burger? You've finally lost some weight, and you know how easy you put it back on."

I took a deep breath in through my nose and out through my mouth. If my mother wasn't complaining about my job, then she was complaining about my weight. As you could imagine, having a fat daughter didn't really fit into her perfect storybook life, and I couldn't count the number of diets or work out plans she had forced me to do over the years. She wanted a daughter who was her mini-me. Someone who she could go to the salon with regularly and dress up like a Barbie doll, but a plus size Barbie wasn't in her repertoire. I was never into sweater vests or pastel pink, and it drove her insane.

"So are you going to tell me the real reason why you wanted to meet today?" I ignored her question about the burger.

"Your father and I have been talking, and we think it's time that you stop playing and decide on a career."

And there it is.

"Your father said that he will allow you to come work at his firm as a receptionist while you get into school, and if you choose an approved major, we'll pay for it."

Now I know what you might be thinking. A free education? Score! But nothing with my parents was free. Everything they gave came with strings attached. Except those strings tended to be more like chains.

Did you hear the "approved" portion of that grand gesture? I knew exactly what that meant. I could choose from being a lawyer, doctor, pharmacist, or a similar career. As if there wasn't anything else that could suck my soul out for cheaper.

I was a creative person. I loved to create, capture, invent, get my hands dirty, and not with a bunch of criminals that I got paid several hundreds of dollars an hour to defend. My dad would defend anyone. As long as you could pay, he'd be on your side.

"That's not going to happen." I shook my head at her. "I have a career, in case I haven't mentioned it before, and I have no interest in going back to school."

"When are you going to stop wasting your life? You have no stability in photography. No guaranteed income."

"It is stable. I'm booked out months at a time."

She waved her hand to cut me off. "What about ten years from now, Kennedy? Do you really think you'll be out there taking pictures?"

I swallowed the words that I wanted to spew at her. I wanted to tell her how happy my photography made me. I wanted her to know how well I was doing, but I knew it wouldn't matter.

I had said it all before and she didn't care.

"Have you talked to Jessica lately?" She stabbed her fork into her salad. "She's almost finished with her MBA."

Internally, I rolled my eyes, but I just dipped a French fry into ketchup.

"She will have so many opportunities when she gets finished. She has so many opportunities in front of her now."

I nodded my head and shoved the fry in my mouth.

It wasn't the first time I had heard about how amazing Jessica was, and it wouldn't be the last.

Jessica's mother and mine had been friends for as long as I could remember, and Jessica had always been around. She was always there, and she had always been better than me. At least to my mother.

She would always be better than me to my mother.

Jessica was the perfect version of the daughter my mother always wanted. She was beautiful, she was smart, she did exactly as her parents wanted, but she was also cruel.

I had spent too many years of my life ridiculed by the cruelty that Jessica spewed.

"That's awesome for her, Mom, but I don't want to get my MBA."

I could see the frustration in her eyes without her even saying a word. I could feel her disappointment.

I'd be lying if I said I hadn't considered it, that I hadn't spent too many nights lying awake in bed thinking about it. About doing whatever it took for them to be proud of me. I thought about it all the time.

"It doesn't have to be your MBA. You have several other options." She smiled a large smile and waved at someone making their way over to us.

And just like that my mother dropped everything else to make small talk with her friend who I didn't recognize. She was dressed almost identically to my mother, and I just smiled and finished my meal while they gossiped.

With every passing second, I let my doubts fester. Doubts about what I was doing. Doubts about whether or not I was making the right decisions.

Doubts about me.

CHAPTER 5

I took my time walking home and took in the scenery around me. Each building, every tree. I imagined how it would look through my camera lens. It calmed me. Centered me. I needed it before I made my way back home. If I had gone home directly from the restaurant, Brooke would have known exactly what was wrong with me, and Brooke despised my parents.

She begged me frequently to quit wasting my time on them at all, but for some reason, I apparently liked to torture myself. I knew the likelihood was practically impossible, but somewhere deep inside of me, I hoped that one day my parents would actually love me for who I was. It was a dream that would never come true, and I needed to stop wasting my time on it. I knew that. But it was easier said than done.

By the time I made it to our building, I was emotional, irritated, and exhausted. A long bubble bath, a large glass of wine, and a good book were exactly what I needed. What I wasn't in the mood for was the loud music that filled the hallway as soon as I made it to our floor.

The sound of me knocking on their door could barely be heard over the music, so I continued to knock until I heard movement from the other side. I never thought I was such a picky neighbor, but the constant noise coming from their apartment was about to drive me insane.

The door jerked open and my jaw hit the floor. In front of me stood a very shirtless and very muscular Tucker. His hands were covered with yellow rubber gloves, and one hand held a bottle of cleaner while the other was latched around a rag.

"What have I done now, Firecracker?"

"Do you need hearing aids?" I dropped my gaze down his tan body tracing the ridges of his abs and practically drooled when I got to the deep V of his hips.

"I don't think so." He chuckled, deep and masculine.

I traced my way back up each ripple of muscle before I noticed he was watching me. My blush was creeping up my chest.

"Well, you're going to if you don't turn down your music. Are you always so loud?"

"I haven't really noticed, but it's good to know that you are noticing me." He smirked, and I simultaneously wanted to suck his bottom lip into my mouth and smack the smirk off his lips.

"I wouldn't take that as a compliment when you're in everyone's face."

"I guess you're right, but Brooke doesn't seem to mind my 'loudness,'" he actually did air quotes, "as much as you do."

He was right, but Brooke rarely complained about anything. It was just who she was.

"I'm really not in the mood for this today, Tucker. Please just turn down the music."

His smirk instantly dropped from his face, and he stood taller.

"Are you okay?" He actually looked concerned.

"Yes. I just need some peace and quiet."

"Done." He looked me in the eyes. "I'll be here for a few more hours before I have to run some errands if you want to talk about it."

"No, thanks." I tucked some loose hair behind my ear. "I'd rather go listen to the characters in my book." I hitched my thumb over my shoulder.

"Well let me know if Fabio has any tips for me." He laughed softly and started to run his gloved hand through his hair but thought better of it.

"Will do." I chuckled, and he smiled at me.

By the time I made it to my door, I could no longer hear the music, and I could kiss Tucker. I liked to think it was only about the music and that it had nothing to do with his pouty lips or scruff on his face. I just needed alone time with a good book to get my head back in line. It would do the trick like nothing else could.

I set my bag down next to the door and Brooke looked up at me from her place on the couch.

"You're home early." I hadn't expected her to be home from work yet. She managed a trendy salon that was just down the road from us, and she absolutely adored her job. It was both great and torturous for me. I got to get my hair done for free by one of the stylists, but Brooke also liked to use me as her dummy for any new products that came in. Sometimes I smelled like a flower bomb blew up in my face. But I couldn't refuse her. I never would.

"I'm actually not. You were gone a really long time." She looked at me concerned.

I looked down at my phone, and I realized that she was right. It had been about two hours since I walked out of the restaurant where my mother sat with her head held high.

"Yeah. I lost track of time."

"How did lunch go?" She watched me like a hawk, and I knew she was looking for any tells on how it really went in case I lied to her about it.

"Same old, same old." I plopped down on the couch beside her, and she pulled me into her side.

"Want to talk about it?"

"Nope."

"Okay. I know I've said this a million times, but you don't need them." Her voice was soft.

I nodded my head at her even though I couldn't really bring myself to believe that deep down.

"We've got each other, and we're all each other will ever need." She pulled me in tighter.

Did I mention that Brooke was the best friend ever? Despite our difference in opinions on clothing, books, style, and who the hottest Hemsworth brother was, I couldn't imagine anyone else being here with me. She was my person in this world.

"I know, babe." I snuggled in tighter against her.

"Now go get one of your books, take a bath, and then we're going out tonight. No arguments."

I swallowed the one that was on the tip of my tongue.

"You don't have a shoot until tomorrow evening, and we need a night out."

"Yes, ma'am." I got up and walked past her to head to the bathroom. She was right. A night out wouldn't hurt us.

"Now that's the attitude I like to see." She slapped my ass and pressed play on her TV show.

She was completely right. We were all each other would ever need.

CHAPTER 6

I was ashamed of myself. Not so ashamed that I probably wouldn't do it again, but the kind of ashamed where I would make the unbreakable vow to never speak about it to anyone.

Everything was going fine. My body was submerged in the hot water, my paperback was perfectly balanced on the side of the tub, and the story I was reading was good. But the sex scenes, they were hot. I could feel a tingle in my stomach when the hero lifted the heroine off the ground and slammed her into the wall, and I decided that was exactly what I needed. To be slammed. But of course, as slightly anti-social and completely single, my chances of that happening at the moment were pretty slim.

So I took the problem into my own hands.

Literally.

I closed my eyes as my hand slid down my body, and I imagined the hero's light blond hair as he threw me on the bed and had his dirty way with me. It was perfect. My stomach tightened as I imagined my hand as his. I sped up as my imagination did.

Then it all went downhill.

The hero's hair changed from the perfect sun-kissed blond to a light brown. His bright blue eyes morphed into a dark brown shade, and somehow it managed to get so much hotter.

If I had any sense whatsoever, I would have stopped what I was doing and cleared my head. But I was too far gone, and apparently, Tucker was going to be the guy to take me to the end.

My body lost control as I imagined his hands running down my body, his scruffy facial hair dragging against my skin. I could see his satisfied smirk in my head when he successfully got me off, and once again I had mixed emotions. I wanted to kill him, slap myself, and then beg him to do it again.

I sank my head under the water, the warmth covering my already overheated body, and I screamed out my frustration. Clearly, self-care wasn't the best option for relieving my stress today. It seemed to make me crazier.

When I got out of the bath, Brooke was waiting for me in my bedroom. She was sitting on my bed acting innocent, but I knew the look on her face.

"Hell no." I pointed straight at her while holding my towel up with my other hand.

"Why not?" She pouted.

"Because I'm not a Barbie."

"I know you're not a Barbie, but it's not a sin to let me do your makeup, you wench."

I smiled at her insult.

"What do I get out of it?"

"To look extra gorgeous tonight." She smiled.

"Try again."

"You can choose what we watch next movie night." She knew she had me with that one and you could see the victory all over her face.

"Deal." I huffed before plopping down at my vanity like a brat. "But don't make me look like a slut."

She put her hand over her heart like that would somehow make her innocent. "Me?"

"Yes. You." I looked at her through the mirror. "I know your makeup bag is filled with slut dust. You sprinkle that crap around like you're a fairy and poof! Sluts everywhere."

"Glitter is not slut dust."

"Whatever you say, slut dust master."

...

By the time everything was said and done, my hair and makeup looked awesome. She lined my green eyes with a sharp, black liner that winged out at the edges and created a sultry effect on my eyes. The rest of my makeup was light except for the bright red lip that, despite my doubts, looked awesome with my hair and light skin tone. She piled my hair on top of my head in a large bun that made me happy because I wouldn't have to deal with it all night.

I put on a Brooke approved pair of black skinny jeans, a white V-neck T-shirt, and a pair of Brooke's black sparkly sandals. I drew the line at heels. Especially if I wanted to make it through the night.

The bar that we chose was pretty packed, but we still managed to get a seat at the bar. The place was ordinary. Nothing special. Just a hole in the wall place where people came to drown their sorrows or drown themselves between each other's legs.

Brooke ordered a martini, and I ordered a whiskey sour. Somehow our drink choices seemed to fit our personalities perfectly. I looked around the bar and watched the people around me. It was an ordinary night with ordinary people.

The guy to my right was leaned into the pretty blonde sitting on the stool who was clearly giving him the "Fuck off" vibes. He either didn't have a clue or didn't care. I wasn't sure which was worse.

The hottest guy in the bar had already saddled up next to Brooke, and she was giggling and throwing him her flirty eyes. And yes. Flirty eyes are a real thing. Not all women are accomplished in the art, take me for example, but Brooke was the master. She could bat her eyelashes a few times and men were eating out of the palm of her hand. I was in awe of her skill.

Just watching her made me smile.

"Hey there, hot stuff." I heard a voice call from behind me.

Please don't be talking to me. Please don't be talking to me. Please don't be talking to me.

The man leaned against the bar and stared at me expectantly.

"I'm sorry?" I asked before taking a sip of my drink.

"What's your name?" He moved in closer to me and beer sloshed out the side of his glass.

"My name is Kennedy."

"Kennedy." He rolled my name over his tongue. "That's a good name. I could see myself calling it out."

"Did you seriously just say that?" I looked around me as if I was being punked.

A snort came from my side, and I turned to see Brooke trying to hide her laughter.

"What? You're not interested in knowing my name? Don't you want to know what it would feel like to scream it out?"

His stale breath blew in my face and I fought the urge to retch. I didn't know if it was from the smell or from his words.

"What's your name?"

He was drunk, and I could see the fuzziness in his vision.

"Brad." He took another sip of his beer. "Do you want to get out of here?"

"Sorry. That's not going to happen." I shook my head softly.

"You don't have to be a bitch." He snarled up his nose. "You're not that good looking anyway."

I pretended like his words didn't hurt me.

He brushed against my side, and I clearly heard the "slut" he tried to say under his breath.

It was the exact reason I wasn't the bar scene kind of girl. I wasn't into empty compliments, if that's what you want to call it, or the empty hookups.

It was the lack of expectation and romance. I wanted sweet words, passionate touches, and grand gestures. I needed to be swept off my feet, not expected to drop to them and open my mouth as soon as I met a guy.

Instead of letting the jerk get to me, I ordered another drink and turned toward my best friend.

"Why are guys so sleazy?" She wrinkled up her nose.

"It's not all guys. At least I don't think so. It just seems to be the men in this bar."

"What's your idea of a perfect guy?" She practically sighed as she said it.

"Well he has to be hot, preferably a six pack, sweeps me off my feet, is alpha enough to piss me off just a little bit, and then he will fuck me like a champion and make it all better again."

"You just described one of your book boyfriends," she said blankly.

"I know and wouldn't it be wonderful if one of them were real." I fanned myself dramatically.

"I think you need to quit reading and get out more. You might actually find a guy that interests you." Her eyes were searching the bar looking for a victim.

"Or maybe you should read more and then you wouldn't have such low standards."

She stuck her tongue out at me, and I laughed.

"You know I'm not a reader. If I was though, I would start with Pride and Prejudice. Mr. Darcy is dreamy."

"You got that right, babe. He is the king of angst."

"Well, I say since there are obviously no Mr. Darcy's in this place, we should drink our fill then go back home and watch him be amazing."

"That sounds like the best plan you've had all day." I raised my glass to hers and we toasted to Mr. Darcy and the unrealistic expectations he gave us.

Brooke and I managed to consume way too many alcoholic beverages, and by the time we made it back to our apartment and started Pride and Prejudice, we were a giggling hot mess. Wine was consumed and our worries went out the window.

When I finally climbed into bed in the early hours of the morning, all concerns regarding my mother were gone, and all that was left were thoughts of Tucker. I had been trying to clear him out of my head as well, but there was something about knowing that he was lying in a bed just behind the thin wall behind me that just wouldn't budge. I was still reeling from my earlier lapse of judgment in the bathtub, but something deep inside my gut was telling me how much I loved the thoughts of him. I completely blamed it on the alcohol and his abs.

I mean did he really have to have abs like that. And that V cut. That was just ridiculous. Nobody really needed that. The only thing it was really good for was tracing it with your tongue. It was really just a cocky display to even have it, but God, I loved it. The urge to run my tongue over his entire body was fierce, and I needed to snap myself out of it.

My body was on fire, but I refused to give into it. One Tucker masturbation a day was all I was allowing myself. I was drawing the line there because clearly, my libido was needing some ground rules.

THANK YOU

Thank you so much for reading Frankie and Olly's story! I cannot thank you enough for reading and loving this series as much as I do!

I would love for you to join my reader group, Hollywood, so we can connect and talk about all of your Boys of Clermont Bay thoughts. This group is the first place to find out about cover reveals, book news, and new releases!

You can also sign up for my newsletter here at www. authorhollyrenee.com/subscribe.

Again, thank you for going on this journey with me.

Xo,

Holly Renee
www.authorhollyrenee.com

Before You Go
Please consider leaving an honest review.

ALSO BY HOLLY RENEE

Stars and Shadows Series:

A Kingdom of Stars and Shadows

A Kingdom of Blood and Betrayal

A Kingdom of Venom and Vows

The Good Girls Series:

Where Good Girls Go to Die

Where Bad Girls Go to Fall

Where Bad Boys are Ruined

The Boys of Clermont Bay Series:

The Touch of a Villain

The Fall of a God

The Taste of an Enemy

The Deceit of a Devil

The Seduction of Pretty Lies

The Temptation of Dirty Secrets

The Rock Bottom Series:

Trouble with the Guy Next Door

Trouble with the Hotshot Boss

Trouble with the Fake Boyfriend

The Wrong Prince Charming

ABOUT THE AUTHOR

USA Today Bestselling Author, Holly Renee brings readers a pinch of angst, an indulgence of heat, and the perfect amount of heart in every book.

Born and raised in East Tennessee, she is a married mom of two wild children. When she's not writing, you can find her reading, pretending to be a dragon for the hundredth time that day, being disgustingly in love with her husband, or chilling in the middle of the lake with her sunglasses and a float.

Holly is a lover of all things romance, Mexican food and yoga pants.

SOCIAL LINKS

authorhollyrenee.com

Instagram: @authorhollyrenee

TikTok: @authorhollyrenee

Facebook Reader Group: Hollywood (Holly Renee's Reader Group)